"I know what you're thinking, Rita, but I won't hurt you again, I promise."

She turned to him. "I'd like to believe that, Erik. But we didn't handle things so well before."

"I know. But that was my fault. I mean it. I want you to trust me. It's not often a person gets a second chance to make things right. Believe me, I don't want to blow it."

"Things seem to be moving so fast. I'm still not sure this is right."

"Maybe I'll just have to convince you all over again, then."

When he looked at her like that, how could she doubt him? And when he took her into his arms, how could she resist? Caught in a sudden wave of longing for him, she leaned against him. He held her tightly, burying his nose in her hair. As they stood there in silence, she could feel him beginning to tremble with the same passion that was rising in her. His face was half in shadow, half in wavering light, and her breath caught as she saw the heat of the desire burning there.

"Tell me now," he said hoarsely. "Because if I kiss you again, I won't be able to stop...."

Weddings by De Wilde™

Weddings by DeWilde™

PREVIOUSLY AT DeWILDES

The House of DeWilde is in turmoil...

- A decades-old marriage has turned sour, and the marital and business partnership between Grace and Jeffrey DeWilde has been severed.
- While Jeffrey makes a go of keeping the London operation afloat alone, Grace has decamped for her native San Francisco, and new opportunities to put her unique retailing stamp on a store of her own.
- Gabriel DeWilde, scion of the DeWilde dynasty, has fallen in love with Lianne, a designer of bridal headdresses employed by the store. But they've cheated Grace and Jeffrey of the chance to use their talents and resources for creating the perfect wedding because...
- they've just eloped!

And now, on to San Francisco....

ISBN 0-373-82538-2

THE RELUCTANT BRIDE

Copyright © 1996 by Harlequin Books S.A.

The Reluctant Bride
JANIS FLORES

Harlequin Books

TORONTO • NEW YORK • LONDON
AMSTERDAM • PARIS • SYDNEY • HAMBURG
STOCKHOLM • ATHENS • TOKYO • MILAN
MADRID • WARSAW • BUDAPEST • AUCKLAND

FROM THE DESK OF
Kate DeWilde

Dear Mother,

I'm sorry it's taken so long to get back to you. I've been so busy with work at the hospital and the clinic that I just haven't had time—no, that's not true. The real reason you haven't heard from me is that, like everyone else who knows and loves you, I'm still in shock about you and Dad. I've read your letter about a million times now, and I guess that on one level I understand that sometimes two people simply must...part. BUT NOT WHEN THOSE TWO PEOPLE ARE MY PARENTS!

I might as well just confess all. Since you're in San Francisco, and on my turf now, so to speak, Gabe and Megan have graciously delegated me to the task of "trying to talk some sense" into you. I know you'll find that as repugnant as I do, but I did promise—only because they're as worried and concerned as I am. So...can we meet for lunch sometime next week? Apart from everything else, I miss you. It will be so wonderful to see you again!

Love,

Kate

CHAPTER ONE

RITA SHANNON WAS LATE. She hated to be late for anything, much less for something as important as this appointment with Grace DeWilde. She also hated to be rushed, and as she practically ran down the long corridor of the San Francisco apartment building, where they had agreed to meet, she caught a glimpse of her reflection in an ornate mirror and grimaced. She should have worn anything else but this insipid green thing that made her skin look sallow.

It was too late to worry about her clothes. She had already changed five times as it was, starting with a red suit, moving on to a dress with a blazer, following that with city shorts, then trying on a plain black outfit that made her look like an undertaker. She'd finally settled on the green—not because she was running out of wardrobe, but because she was running out of time.

Now she was almost five minutes behind schedule. What was Grace DeWilde going to think?

She was going to think that Rita Shannon had some nerve applying for the job of executive assistant. Rita debated about reversing course, going back down to the front desk, asking for a phone and canceling the appointment—only to wonder: *Are you nuts?*

How could she even think of giving up a chance to meet—no, to work with—a woman she had admired ever since she'd taken a course on Women in Business at college? She'd made Grace DeWilde the subject of a term paper for that class and had received an A. But even more important, she had also discovered an idol, a woman to emulate. She'd wanted to be just like Grace.

Her mouth tightened. Things hadn't worked out quite the way she'd planned, which was why she was racing down this hallway now, late for an appointment that was probably going to be the most important in her life.

Things happen for the best.

Did they? she wondered. Her mother was always saying that, and sometimes she believed it was true. The ironic twist about today was that she wouldn't be here if she hadn't lost her job at Maxwell and Company, the San Francisco-based department store.

Well, she hadn't *lost* her job. The truth was, she'd quit—about two seconds before she'd been fired. Still, it was a source of great satisfaction that she had walked out on her boss, a pompous idiot named Gerald Hastings who hadn't the vision of a gnat.

"I don't see what the problem is, Gerald," she'd said on her last morning at Maxwell's. She'd been doing her best to remain calm—always an iffy proposition with her volatile temper—because the topic had been important to her. But she and Gerald, who was head buyer, had been discussing her bridal boutique idea for almost an hour, and she hadn't made any headway at all.

In fact, she had realized impatiently, she was probably further away from convincing him than when she'd walked through his office door.

Gerald had regarded her with distaste. He was the boss's nephew, and he never let anyone forget it.

"I told you, Rita," he'd said with that patronizing tone that drove her wild, "bridal departments are too expensive. The overhead is too high and the profit margin too low. We've already discussed it.''

She couldn't help herself. The man obviously hadn't read her carefully prepared proposal. ''If you'll reread the figures I collected for you, you'll see that—''

''I don't have to read them. The answer is no.''

''I don't believe you've thought this through,'' she'd said between clenched teeth. ''I'm not asking for much space, just enough to display some gowns and veils, a few pairs of shoes and of course lingerie. We don't have to add linens or china and crystal, or even jewelry…yet. I know it will work if we just give it a shot.''

''Didn't you hear what I just said?''

She'd wanted to jump over the desk, grab his lapels and give him the shaking he so richly deserved! But she refused to jeopardize her chances. The bridal department meant everything to her, and she was going to fight for it. ''Yes, I heard you. But I'm sure that once you realize—''

''As usual, I don't believe we're communicating, Rita. So let me put it as clearly as I can. A bridal boutique at Maxwell and Company is out of the question. We don't need it, and I don't want it.''

They glared at each other, and Rita knew there was nothing more she could do to try to convince this visionless little man. The realization made her so angry that she said, ''Well, fine, Gerald. But maybe it's not your decision to make.''

He'd stiffened. ''Are you implying that you'd go over my head?''

''I'm not *implying* anything.''

''I'm not sure I like your tone.''

Her big mouth had always gotten her into trouble. Before she knew it, she shot back, ''And I'm *certain* I don't like yours. So why don't we take this up with Mr. Rossmore?''

Gerald's face reddened at her mention of the store manager. "I think you've forgotten that you're only my assistant!''

Rashly, she said, "How could I forget? You remind me of it at every opportunity!''

"Not anymore! Because as of this moment, you're—''

"Wait a minute!''

He was actually going to *fire* her, after all she'd done for this store? The only reason she'd stayed on after the takeover was because of promises made by the new management—promises that had never been fulfilled. She'd been a fool to believe a word from people who had destroyed an institution like Glencannon's just for a bigger share of the market. She should never have given a minute of her time to Jason Maxwell and his looters, no matter what they had said to her. It had been lies, all lies.

She looked at Gerald Hastings. When she saw his expression, she knew he expected her to apologize, but she'd be damned if she'd give him the satisfaction.

"You can't fire me, Gerald," she'd said, as calm as could be outwardly, while inside her heart was pounding. What was she doing? Who quit a job without having another lined up?

"Oh, no?" he smirked.

"No," she'd declared. "I *quit*.''

What a fine moment that had been! she thought now. She'd jerked the door open and walked out to—a month of unemployment.

Finally, she spied the number the employment agency had given her for Grace DeWilde's apartment. Her pulse racing, she stopped outside the door to catch her breath. She was so nervous she could hardly remember her own name. In sudden panic, she knew she was going to make some incredible gaffe. Grace DeWilde was going to take one look at her and say something to the effect—

"Stop it!" she commanded herself fiercely. She was getting into a state for no reason at all. She had to remember her qualifications. She could do this job; all she needed was a chance to prove it. Lifting her hand, she rapped firmly on the door. It opened, and before she knew it, she was face-to-face with her idol.

She would have recognized Grace DeWilde anywhere, she thought; she looked just like all the pictures Rita had seen in the numerous magazines that followed her career. But to meet her in person—to actually see that Grace DeWilde's blond hair was just as perfectly coiffed as it appeared in print, the famous blue eyes just as clear and the figure in the powder blue suit just as slender—was so impressive that, for a moment, Rita could only stand there staring.

Then she realized that she hadn't said anything yet, and that Grace DeWilde was gazing at her questioningly. Pulling herself together, she said, "Mrs. DeWilde? I'm Rita Shannon. The Summit Agency sent me."

Grace DeWilde smiled warmly and held out her hand. "Hello, Rita. Welcome."

And just like that, she was in, following the icon into the front room. A silver tea service was arranged on the low coffee table between a sofa and a chair, and Grace gestured her to a seat before taking one herself behind the elaborate tray.

"I was just about to have a cup of tea," Grace said. "Would you care for one? Or, if you prefer, I can make coffee."

Wondering if she'd be able to swallow over the nervous lump in her throat, Rita said, "Tea would be fine, thank you."

As she watched Grace pour, her long-fingered hands with the manicured nails moving so elegantly, Rita took another deep breath to calm herself. She'd heard of hero—or rather, heroine—worship, but she was being ridiculous. She, who was *never* at a loss for words in practically any situation, felt numb and tongue-tied, and if she didn't snap out of it, this woman was going to think she was a complete idiot.

"Sugar? Milk? Lemon?" Grace asked. Despite living in England all these years, she had just the merest trace of a British accent, which gave a charming lilt to her low, husky voice.

"Nothing, thank you," Rita said. Although she usually liked her tea sweetened, she was too nervous to risk fumbling with a spoon and sugar bowl. She accepted the cup Grace handed her and, after taking a sip, managed by sheer concentration to set it down on the coffee table without sloshing any tea onto the saucer.

As Grace poured a cup for herself, Rita studied her idol. She decided then that the pictures she'd seen didn't do the woman justice. In all those newspaper photos and magazine articles, Grace DeWilde looked austere, remote, almost untouchable even when she smiled. But in person, she was much warmer, more vibrant and alive.

Rita caught sight of her briefcase by her feet and realized that she hadn't handed over her résumé yet. Quickly she reached for the attaché and took out the folder she had carefully prepared. Even though she'd been proud of the contents last night when she checked it for mistakes, it seemed totally inadequate now. But she couldn't pretend she didn't have it, so she said, "I brought a copy of my résumé."

Grace barely glanced at it. She took a sip of the fragrant tea—it had to be a special blend, Rita thought distractedly, for she hadn't recognized the taste or the scent—and said, "Thank you, but I've already seen it. The agency sent me résumés of all the applicants for the job."

All the applicants? How many were there? Instantly, Rita felt another surge of anxiety that she strangled by pure will. It didn't matter that, at the moment, everyone in the world seemed more competent than she did. What was important was that no one could possibly want this position more. It was up to her to convince Grace DeWilde that she was the woman for the job.

"I see," she said. "Well, then, in that case, I assume you'll be quite busy interviewing. You must have questions, so if I can explain or add to the information you already have, I'll be happy to do so."

Grace smiled. When Rita saw the amusement in her eyes, she wanted to kick herself. In her eagerness to convince Grace that she was the right choice for assistant, she had taken over—or tried to—this interview. Well, that was like her, she thought, resigning herself to being shown the door. She'd always had an attitude. Or, in the words of one of her brothers, she was a decisive, opinionated, take-charge personality with a big mouth.

"I meant—" she started to say.

Grace put down her cup with another smile. "I know what you mean. And I applaud your desire not to waste time."

Thank God, Rita thought.

"Because," Grace went on, "I'm exactly the same way myself. I've found, over the years, that's the only way to get things done."

Feeling reprieved, Rita said, "Obviously, I agree."

Grace regarded her thoughtfully for a moment. "I know by your résumé that you're qualified for this position. In fact, from what I've read, you seem to be overqualified for the job. I believe at one point you were head buyer at... I'm sorry, which store was it?"

"Glencannon's," Rita said, and was instantly thrown back in time to that awful period of her life when she'd lost not only her job, but a relationship that she'd once thought would lead to marriage. An image of a man's handsome face took shape in her mind, but she furiously willed it away. She didn't want to think of Erik Mulholland now, of all times. In fact, she never wanted to think of him again.

"I remember now," Grace said. "Glencannon's was one of San Francisco's most venerable department stores, and it was taken over by the larger Maxwell and Company, wasn't it?"

"Yes, it was." Rita's jaw tightened and her voice took on an edge. "Glencannon's was merged into Maxwell and Company last year. It was a hostile takeover, and a lot of us were caught right in the middle of it."

Grace looked sympathetic. "That seems to be more of a common experience today than many people realize. I'm sure it was difficult for you."

Difficult? Rita thought. She supposed she could call it that. With ambitions to be an executive one day, she'd begun on the lowest rung at Glencannon's, starting at minimum wage as a salesclerk. She had worked her way up to head of her department, women's fashion, then to assistant buyer and finally to head buyer. She would have risen higher, she knew, but things changed. Erik Mulholland came onto the scene, and before anyone knew it, they were taking down the old Glencannon's sign and putting up one from Maxwell and Company in its place.

Rita could still remember that last awful day. The owner of the store, a wonderful man named Harvey Glencannon, had personally come around to all the employees to say goodbye. It was all Rita could do not to burst into tears when he shook her hand and thanked her for all she'd done for him and the store. She'd never seen anyone look so old and defeated. It was enough to break her heart...and it had all been Erik Mulholland's fault.

How clever Erik had been! she thought. Effortlessly, he had penetrated her defenses. He had made her fall in love with him, he had engaged her in their torrid, passionate affair. But he had never been in love with her; she'd just been a convenient source to pump for information he could use to engineer the takeover.

And she'd had her comeuppance for her lack of discretion. Mr. Glencannon had tried to ensure that most of his employees retained their positions with the new owners, but it wasn't long before they all had a nasty shock. Some, even longtime workers, had been let go immediately by the new owners. Others had been told to transfer or else. And a few had been demoted, just as she'd been.

The new people had told her that they had complete confidence in her. In fact, they were certain that soon she'd have enough expertise to be a head buyer in the new store. But until that time, she just didn't have the experience that a national chain like Maxwell's required. While she learned the ropes, Gerald Hastings was going to take over the head buyer's office. She would be his assistant. It was only temporary—so they'd said.

She couldn't go into that with Grace DeWilde now, so all she said was "Yes, it was difficult, especially when I was demoted to assistant buyer after the takeover. I stuck it out as long as I could, but finally my boss and I came to... a parting of the ways."

"I see. Would you like to tell me about it?"

Trying to downplay it, Rita said, "There's not much to tell. I wanted to open a bridal boutique in the store, and he... didn't."

"And you left over that?"

"That was the excuse, I guess. But things hadn't been going well since the takeover. I just didn't like the store after Mr. Glencannon left. It was time for a change."

"And so now you want to be an executive assistant."

"Not just anyone's executive assistant," Rita said honestly. "Yours."

When Grace looked both surprised and amused, Rita leaned forward. Although her entire future wasn't tied up with getting this job, it seemed like it, and she *was* determined. "I don't mean to gush, but I've admired you and followed your career for years, Mrs. DeWilde. I even wrote a term paper on you in college."

Grace put a hand to her throat. "My goodness."

"I know how that sounds," Rita said. "But the truth is that you've been a model and an inspiration to me. After what's happened the past few years, I admit I'm behind schedule careerwise, but my ambition is to be an executive myself one day, and I can't think of a better way to learn, or a better teacher than you."

She sat back. While she waited nervously, wondering if she had overplayed it, or sounded as if she were trying to curry favor, Grace DeWilde regarded her thoughtfully. Then Grace said, "As I mentioned, the agency gave me several candidates for the job, but I don't think further interviews will be necessary. I mentioned a salary to the agency—"

"I know, and it's very generous, Mrs. DeWilde."

"Then, if you find that acceptable, and if you want it, the job is yours."

If she wanted it? She started to answer, but Grace held up a hand.

"Before you say anything, perhaps I should explain my plans. Do you understand that, no matter what your decision is after this, our discussion does not go beyond this room?"

Rita would have gone to the rack before breathing a word. "Of course."

Grace nodded. "Since you have so flatteringly indicated that you've followed my career, perhaps you're aware that I am no longer associated with the DeWilde Corporation. My husband and I are...separated."

Rita knew all about it—or at least what she could glean from following the story in the media. Carefully, she said, "I've read about it."

"Without going into all the boring details, the crux of it is that I came back to San Francisco to open my own store."

It was what Rita had been hoping for. "Another DeWilde's!" she breathed.

"In a way," Grace said. "I've wanted to do this for a long time. But this store will be slightly different. It will be more...San Francisco, if you know what I mean."

Rita was sure that she knew exactly what Grace meant. Barely able to suppress her excitement, she thought of the ideas she had presented to Gerald Hastings and sent up a silent thanks that he had rejected them. She'd been so down when she quit; she'd thought life was over. But a whole new world was opening up to her, and she had Gerald's narrow-minded shortsightedness to thank.

Things happen for the best. Hadn't her mother told her that a thousand times? *Well, Mom,* she thought giddily, *I can't wait to tell you how right you were!*

Hardly daring to believe her good fortune, she said, "When do we start?"

"How about tomorrow?"

"Why wait?" Rita said gaily. She was eager to begin immediately, before Grace changed her mind.

Her new employer laughed. "I do value enthusiasm, and ordinarily I'd take you up on the offer because we have so much to do to get ready. But I have a few calls to make this afternoon—one of which is to someone who can help with the financial and legal aspects of the new store."

"I can make those calls for you," Rita said eagerly.

Grace laughed again. "Thank you, but I think I'd better do it myself."

"Is there anything else I can do?"

"You can be here at nine sharp tomorrow morning."

Rita was so thrilled that she'd actually gotten the job that she wanted to dance around the room. Instead, she made herself reach decorously for her purse and briefcase. She stood and held out her hand.

"Thank you for this opportunity, Mrs. DeWilde."

Grace took her hand with a smile and a wry warning. "Don't thank me. I expect a lot from my assistants."

Rita couldn't hide her grin any longer. Her dark eyes sparkling, she said, "I won't let you down, I promise."

She couldn't stop smiling, not even when she entered the elevator with a half dozen other people. She didn't care that they all looked at her and then quickly away, as if afraid she were on something. Well, she was, she thought delightedly. Long before she reached ground level, she was on cloud nine.

CHAPTER TWO

CAROLINE MADISON SMILED at Erik Mulholland during lunch on the same day that Rita was hired by Grace DeWilde. Eric had taken her to a new restaurant called Patisse, and she reached across the table and placed one delicate hand over his. In the muted light, her perfectly manicured nails gleamed a pale pink. The color matched her designer suit, as well as her lipstick, her nylons and her heels. In fact, the only things about her that weren't pink today were her blue eyes and pale blond hair.

And the large amethyst ring surrounded by diamonds that she was wearing on the ring finger of her left hand, Erik realized with a grimace. He hadn't given her that particular piece of jewelry, and when he saw it glaring almost accusingly at him, he quickly glanced away.

"I was so surprised when you called and asked me to lunch today," Caroline said. "I know how busy you are, darling. And we *are* going to have dinner tonight with Mother and Daddy."

Erik put down the wine list he'd been studying. Reluctantly, he decided that he didn't need anything to drink right now. Some important clients were coming to the office this afternoon and he had to be clearheaded and in top form. They were an Asian group who wanted him to put together a deal for yet another hotel in the center of San Francisco; if he could swing it, the commission would go a long way toward alleviating his guilt about adding to the city's clutter. In his opinion, San Francisco needed another mammoth hotel like it needed a new crime wave.

"I know," he said. "But I wanted to see you."

"I would be flattered if you didn't sound so serious. Is everything all right?"

He wasn't sure. It wasn't like him to be impulsive, but when he'd called to ask her to lunch this morning, it was because today was the day he'd finally decided to propose. He had to do it before he thought any more about it or he'd change his mind again. It had happened to him before: he'd get right to the brink, but he couldn't make himself jump off.

It seemed he couldn't jump today, either. The ring was in his pocket, but now that the time was here, he couldn't say the words. He didn't know why; every time he looked at her, he told himself he was damned lucky to have a woman like Caroline Madison in love with him.

But was he in love with her? He thought he was—no, he was *certain* he was. But if that were so, what kept him tongue-tied when he should be proposing with a glass of champagne?

Caroline was gazing at him with a slight frown of concern, and once again, he thought how beautiful she was. Everything about her was perfect: her blond, blue-eyed WASP good looks; a bloodline on the Madison side that went all the way back to the *Mayflower;* even her choice of designer wardrobe, understated and chic. He had never seen her flustered or out of sorts; in fact, he didn't believe that he had ever heard her raise her voice. She loved children and volunteered her time once a week at a day-care center on Nob Hill whose waiting list was two years' long. She was everything he was supposed to want, and yet . . .

"Everything's fine," he said, the ring in its box feeling like a ton of lead in his pocket—where it seemed it was going to stay, at least for today. He reached for her hand. "I'm sorry. I asked you to lunch, and now I'm poor company."

She gave him a dazzling smile that made him wonder again why he didn't grab the opportunity to make her his wife. "You're never poor company, Erik. It's just that I worry about you. I know you work too hard."

"Don't be silly," he said. "Besides, I enjoy my work."

"Do you?" Her eyes searched his face. "Sometimes I wonder. Especially lately. You just haven't seemed to be yourself. Are you worried about something?"

"No, of course not. Maybe I have too much on my mind."

Caroline hesitated, then she asked, "Is one of those things my father's offer?"

Caroline's father was Niles Madison. Although Niles was semiretired now, he still kept an office at the blue-blood investment firm of Morton, Madison and Shade. Recently, Niles had dangled a vice presidency under Erik's nose. It was a plum beyond belief, something that would set Erik up for life. He knew he should have jumped at it, but he didn't like the feeling he was being bribed. Oh, nothing overt had been said, nothing had even been implied. But he'd been around; he knew that Caroline came with that vice presidency. So he'd told Niles he had to think about it. He'd thought about almost nothing else since.

But that didn't mean he wanted to talk about it. "Now, Caroline, we agreed—"

"I know, I know," she said with a sigh. "I realize you have to make up your own mind."

Now he felt guiltier than ever. "It's not that I don't appreciate it, because I do. It's just that I have Rudy to consider. We've worked hard to build our own investment firm, and I can't just leave him in the lurch."

"Rudy may be your partner at Mulholland-Laughton, but he's a big boy," Caroline said with an edge to her voice that sometimes crept in when she wasn't careful. "He can take care of himself."

Erik didn't want to discuss it. Trying to lighten the mood, he said, "That's true. After all, he's a lawyer."

Caroline didn't smile with him. Reaching for her water glass, she said, "I hope you won't take too long making up your mind, Erik. Daddy made a generous offer, I think, and you owe it to him to reply."

"You're right, and I will—when the time comes." He changed the subject by asking, "In the meantime, what would you like for dessert?"

"Nothing, thank you," Caroline replied. She looked at her watch and frowned. "Oh, dear. I was supposed to be at that fitting ten minutes ago. Would you mind if we just got the check?"

He didn't mind at all; in fact, he was relieved. Outside, he gave her a brief kiss goodbye before gesturing for a cab. As one started toward them, he asked, "Are you angry with me?"

She thought a moment, then shook her head. "No, but it is difficult. Daddy keeps asking me if you've made a decision. He has such hopes . . ." She looked up at him before adding, "And so do I."

He didn't know what to say. Fortunately the cab pulled up to the curb just then, and he was able to forgo a reply by opening the door and helping her in.

"I'll see you tonight," he said lamely, wishing he could promise more.

"Yes, we'll talk then."

It was his turn to sigh as the cab pulled away. He stared after it for a few seconds, then he headed back to his office on Kearny.

The investment firm of Mulholland-Laughton was on the twentieth floor of the Vale building. When he got there, his secretary, Eleanor, was still out to lunch. Down the hall, Rudy's door was open, which meant his partner was out, too. It was just as well, Erik thought. He didn't feel like talking to anyone right now. Preoccupied, he walked into his own office, but instead of getting down to work, he went to stand by the window behind his desk.

What was the matter with him? Why didn't he just ask Caroline to marry him and get it over with? Something was holding him back, but what? Soon he'd be forty years old; it was past time to settle down and start a family. If he wasn't careful, he'd sacrifice everything to his work, even his love life.

His love life.

Out of the blue, a face flashed through his mind—a delicate oval face with expressive wide brown eyes and a mobile, sensual mouth.

Damn it! he thought. Where had that come from? He'd trained himself not to think of Rita Shannon. Why had she entered his mind today?

But he knew why he'd thought of Rita, and it wasn't just because of the passionate affair they'd had last year. He'd been thinking of how much he'd sacrificed to his work, and Rita had been one of the casualties. At one point, he'd been so crazy in love with her that he'd almost asked her to marry him.

He was glad that he hadn't. Once their blistering affair was over and he'd had time to analyze things, he knew the marriage would never have worked. Rita wasn't the kind of woman he needed; she never would have fit into his plans. She'd been too opinionated, too irrepressible, too...vibrant. If she didn't like something, she said so—in no uncertain terms. She'd offer her opinion whether you wanted it or not. It just wasn't in her to become a corporate, play-by-the-rules wife.

And a corporate wife was what he wanted, he assured himself. He needed a woman who would be an asset—not only to his career, but to his peace of mind. He knew that made him the worst kind of chauvinist, and he was sorry, but that's the way it had to be. His work was high-profile and extremely demanding, and because of that, he had to have a wife with no career aspirations herself. He needed someone who understood about all the hours spent at the office; someone who wouldn't complain if he missed a birthday or anniversary or other occasion he'd promised to attend but couldn't. In short, he thought with another wince, what he needed was a "traditional" wife.

He almost laughed. Rita Shannon was the last woman to fit into the traditional mold. Almost as ambitious and driven as he was, she'd been head buyer at Glencannon's department store when they first met. But she'd had even higher aspirations, and had made no secret of it.

But then, as often happened in the world of corporate takeovers, Glencannon's was no more, having been absorbed by Maxwell and Company.

People had gotten rich off that deal, Erik remembered with a tightening of his jaw. But though he'd been involved until almost the very end, he hadn't been one of them. In their last quarrel, Rita had accused him of engineering the whole thing, but he couldn't explain what had really happened—not that it mattered by that time. Feelings were so bitter between them that no explanation on his part would have healed their rift.

He was still standing by the window, staring out at nothing, when Eleanor came in.

"Erik?"

"Yes, what is it?" he asked, turning away from the view of the bridge he hadn't even seen. It took him a moment to realize that his normally unflappable secretary looked excited.

"I'm sorry to disturb you," Eleanor said, "but Grace DeWilde is on the phone. She said she'd make an appointment, but I thought you'd want to speak to her yourself."

Grace DeWilde? he thought, startled. Of course he knew who she was—who didn't? Last month, around the first of May, she and her husband had announced their separation; ever since, the business and financial communities had buzzed about the consequences.

And consequences there would inevitably be, Erik knew. In his business, it paid to be informed, and he'd followed the developing situation closely. The DeWilde Corporation was still considered family-owned, although some years before, they'd had to raise capital by floating shares on the New York and London stock exchanges. DeWilde stocks were holding, so far, but Erik knew that if Grace decided to sell her five percent share as a single block, the market value of all the shares would fall like a rock.

He'd heard through the usual sources that Grace DeWilde had returned to San Francisco, so he knew she was in town. Curious as to why she'd be calling him, he grinned at his wide-eyed secretary as he reached for the phone.

"Thanks, Eleanor," he said, "let's see what we can do for her."

He pressed down the blinking button on line one. "Mrs. DeWilde? This is Erik Mulholland. How may I help you?"

A warm, slightly husky voice answered. "I've got a problem, Mr. Mulholland. I'd like to meet and discuss it with you, if you have time."

Erik glanced at his crowded calendar, then swept it aside. Apart from his interest in the problems Grace DeWilde faced right now, he was intrigued about meeting the woman he'd always respected from afar. Even on this side of the Atlantic, her business acumen was renowned, and it was conventional wisdom that much of the success of the DeWilde stores was due to Grace DeWilde's merchandising savvy.

"My time is yours," he said before he saw Eleanor frantically signaling him. "Except for a few minutes this afternoon. Regretfully, I have a prior appointment I can't break."

Her rich voice broke into a laugh that charmed him even more. "I have no intention of wreaking havoc with your schedule," she assured him. "I know only too well how disruptive that can be. In fact, I really intended to go through the channels and make an appointment with your secretary, but she put me through to you before I could protest."

"As well she should have," he said, winking at Eleanor, who reluctantly went out, closing the door behind her. "So, now that that's settled, when would be convenient for you? I would be pleased to meet you at your office—"

"I'm afraid I don't have a formal office—yet. At the moment, I'm using the living room of my apartment. So I think it would be easier all around if I just came to you."

"Name the date and time."

"I know this is short notice, but . . . sometime this week? Say, Wednesday afternoon about three?"

He looked down at his calendar again. Wednesday was completely filled, but he said, "That's fine. I'll expect you then." He hesitated, then had to ask, "In the meantime, if I might have some idea what this is about . . . ? It goes without saying that anything you tell me will remain completely confidential."

"I'm sure," she replied in a tone that indicated she expected no less. She paused. "I've been thinking about opening a new store—here, in San Francisco."

This time, he couldn't conceal his surprise. "Another DeWilde's?"

"Well, this one will be mine alone."

"I see," he said—and he did. His mind was already racing with the implications; he knew now what she wanted from him. "How large do you plan this new store to be?"

"I haven't decided yet. It's one of the things we need to discuss. One among many, I'm afraid," she added. "But we can do that on Wednesday. Oh, yes, and I plan to have my new assistant with me. I hope that won't be a problem?"

He was so intrigued about the possibilities of this venture that he wouldn't have cared if she'd asked to bring her own brass band. Gallantly, he said, "No, not at all."

"Good. Then we'll see you on Wednesday."

"I'll look forward to meeting you both."

Thoughtfully, he said goodbye and hung up the phone. The financial community had been theorizing about what would happen to DeWilde stock if Grace DeWilde opened a rival store. Now, it seemed, they were all about to find out. Suddenly he was anxious for Wednesday to come. It had been a long time since he'd been this energized about a project; maybe this deal with Grace DeWilde would be what he needed, a shot in the arm.

And yet for all the excitement Grace DeWilde's call had generated in him, he found that for the rest of that afternoon, even during his important meeting with the Ishitaki group, he wasn't thinking about business. To his dismay, only one face, one name, one voice kept popping into his head.

Why did Rita matter so much to him after all this time? he finally asked himself in exasperation. Was it because they'd parted on such a bitter note? Maybe he still felt guilty. He wished he'd been more up-front, but what could he do about it now?

It's all in the past, he told himself impatiently. The Glencannon debacle had been the wedge that drove him and Rita apart, but he knew it would have happened, anyway. They were just too different; they had nothing—except physical attraction—in common. So what if he'd loved the way she smiled, or admired her drive and ambition? What difference did it make that he appreciated her quick wit and found her silly jokes funny? Life went on, and despite the ugly way things had ended between them, he'd gone on, too. And he knew she had, as well.

It was over, he told himself. None of it mattered anymore.

But he was still preoccupied with thoughts of Rita as he drove up to the elegant, turn-of-the-century mansion at the top of Russian Hill to have dinner with Caroline and her parents.

"I DON'T THINK you've heard a word I've said all evening," Caroline complained. They had left the table after a meal that Erik couldn't have described if he'd been paid, and were now sitting in the living room. To his relief, Niles and Pamela, Caroline's mother, had excused themselves and disappeared upstairs.

"I'm sorry, Caroline," he said. "It's been a long day."

"Would you like to talk about it?"

Erik was holding a brandy he hadn't wanted but had poured because he'd hoped it would relax him. It hadn't worked; he still felt so tense that it was an effort even to be civil.

"It's nothing," he lied. "Just a problem with a new Asian consortium."

She leaned against him and ran her fingers through his hair. The gesture should have been tender and loving; tonight it irritated the hell out of him, and he grabbed her hand. "I think I should go," he said.

"Oh, not yet! It's so early."

He could smell the sweet scent of her perfume and wanted to move away but made himself sit still. "I know, but I have a lot of work to do tomorrow."

"Erik, we need to talk."

He tensed again. "About what?"

"How would you feel about getting away for a few days? We could go up to the wine country or take a drive up the coast. There are some wonderful bed-and-breakfast places in Mendocino, and we could just relax." She paused significantly. "Just the two of us."

He couldn't imagine why the idea didn't appeal to him.

"It sounds like a wonderful idea, Caroline, but I just can't get away right now."

She pressed against him again. "Please, darling," she whispered. "It's been so long since we've had a chance to be alone."

Gingerly, he put an arm around her. She didn't like to be rumpled, as she put it, and sometimes such gestures annoyed her. Inconveniently, another image flashed into his mind just then, one of Rita in jeans and sweatshirt, running after a dog who'd gotten away from its owner down by the marina. She'd caught the animal by its flapping leash and the two of them had flown along for a distance, Rita laughing in sheer joy, the dog joining in her exuberance.

The thought occurred to him that Caroline would have died before trying on—much less being seen in— jeans. And as for getting near animals, especially big, strange dogs . . .

Irritated that he was thinking of Rita Shannon when beautiful, perfect Caroline was in his arms, he said, "I'll think about it."

She gazed up at him with that adoring look that made him feel secretly a little pleased and annoyed at the same time. "Will you?" she asked.

He felt like a heel. Kissing her briefly, he said, "Of course I will."

He started to get up, but she put her arms around him. "I hope so," she said, gazing into his eyes. "Because it would be so lovely to go away with you, even for a few days."

He started to kiss her again, but once more—damn it—a memory of Rita intruded, the time they had stolen a weekend and flown to Aruba. With that wicked smile of hers, Rita had shown him how quickly she could pack. The string bikini she had taken had fit into a tiny little pouch.

And most of that weekend, he recalled with a twinge that sent the blood rushing to his head—and other regions—she hadn't even bothered with that.

He wanted to kiss Caroline; he wanted to make love to her. But how could he do that when another woman filled his mind? With a feeble excuse, he said his goodbyes and made his way to his car as quickly as he could.

CHAPTER THREE

RITA AND GRACE DEWILDE arrived five minutes early for their three o'clock Wednesday appointment. Grace had told Rita only that they were going to an investment firm for help in financing the new store, and Rita didn't have time to read the occupant listing by the elevator before they were whisked to the twentieth floor. When they stepped out, a swath of elegant dove-gray carpet led them to an office painted in cream and Wedgwood blue, where an efficient receptionist sat behind a desk that looked like a console for the space shuttle. Among the many telephones, fax machines, printers and other paraphernalia was a nameplate that identified the woman as Eleanor Whitley. She had been furiously typing on a keyboard when they came in, but she immediately lifted her hands and smiled at them.

"Good afternoon. You must be Mrs. DeWilde," she said with a nod that included Rita. She reached for a telephone. "I'll tell Mr. Mulholland that you're both here."

Rita had been about to take a seat on one of the two cream-colored sofas in the reception area. She froze at the name. Surely she hadn't heard right, she thought with a flash of alarm. Then, quickly, she told herself that even if she had, there must be dozens of Mullollands in San Francisco. It would be too much of a coincidence for this one to be named Erik.

She'd barely finished the thought before the door to her left opened. She hadn't even had time to prepare herself before she was staring into the dark blue eyes of the man she had vowed to despise for the rest of their natural lives.

For a moment, they both just stood there. Rita couldn't have spoken if she'd tried. How could this have happened? she wondered in a panic. Why hadn't Grace warned her? Why hadn't she asked?

She tried to compose herself. It wasn't Grace's fault. How could she have possibly known that Rita and Erik Mulholland had...a history? Rita was to blame for not finding out who they were coming to see. It was an obvious question, but she'd been so busy working for Grace these past two days that she hadn't had time to wonder. Now what was she going to do?

As always when she felt intimidated or unsure of herself, she took the initiative. Ignoring the fact that her heart had begun to hammer in anticipation of what he might—or might not—say, she held out her hand and said, as cool as could be, "Hello, Erik."

It was a moment before he answered. She was already fantasizing how she would handle it if he fell to his knees in front of her and begged her forgiveness, when he shook her hand perfunctorily and said in that deep voice she still remembered, "Hello, Rita. It's been a long time."

That detached tone did it. *So,* she thought, *that's how it's going to be. Well, fine. Two can play that game.*

"Has it?" she said. "I've been so busy I've lost track."

Erik didn't answer; he just smiled. Then he looked beyond her and said to Grace, "Mrs. DeWilde, it's a pleasure to meet you. Please, come into my office.

Would you care for tea? I have a special blend of Earl Grey that I believe you like...."

Chatting amiably, he took Grace's elbow and led her into the inner sanctum, apparently leaving Rita behind to follow or not. Seething at what seemed to be a deliberate snub, she entered behind them and just barely managed to close the door without giving it a good kick.

Erik was already seating Grace on yet another sofa, this one in a muted blue. He seemed to remember Rita then, and kindly gestured her to a matching chair in a grouping that included a low, circular coffee table. A vast slab of a desk stood at the opposite end of the room; behind it was a huge window that offered a panoramic view of the Golden Gate Bridge. The desk held three telephones, a green onyx desk set, a laptop computer and nothing else.

Rita sat down. On the wall in front of her hung a large abstract painting with great slashes of color and framed in black. It seemed to mirror just how she was feeling right now, and she smiled grimly at it. Then she noticed a magnificent sculpture of an eagle in flight, standing by itself in a corner.

Rita hadn't seen any of these things before, and as she glanced covertly around, she realized that Erik had not only changed the location of his office since she had last seen him, but completely redecorated, too. Grudgingly, she had to admit that it was spectacular. Just as he'd been. The thought immediately annoyed her, and she looked down. When she saw that she was gripping the strap of her purse and the handle of her briefcase so tightly that her fingers were white, she put both of them on the floor.

The secretary knocked, then came in with a tray upon which was a silver service more elaborate than the one

Grace used at the apartment. On the tray were cups and saucers that immediately irritated Rita. She was sure the china was Spode, and of course its pattern of flowers and vines was neither masculine nor feminine, just exquisite. Accompanying the tea was a plate of delicate cookies and another of petits fours.

Trust Erik to have the best, she thought as Eleanor set the tray on the low coffee table. She was so annoyed that she decided he'd probably sent the secretary out to buy the set on the day Grace called for her appointment. He'd always been a detail man, she thought derisively. It was what made him so good at his job.

"You seem to have thought of everything," Grace murmured with frank appreciation after Eleanor had withdrawn, closing the door behind her.

Erik waved away the compliment with one of his devastating smiles. "I wanted you to feel welcome, Mrs DeWilde."

"Grace, please."

"Then you must call me Erik." He gestured. "Would you pour?"

Grace performed the ritual with her usual elegance. Still trying to maintain her composure, Rita accepted her cup but refused anything to eat. Inside, she was fuming. Erik, damn the man, hardly seemed to notice she was here, while *she* seemed all too achingly aware of his every word and gesture.

"We have that information, don't we, Rita?"

Rita realized that both Grace and Erik were looking at her expectantly. She'd been so preoccupied that she hadn't the faintest idea what they'd been talking about. Her cheeks burning at having been caught in such a lapse, she said, "I brought all the relevant papers, Mrs DeWilde."

As though she knew exactly what she was doing, she set aside her untouched cup of tea and reached for her briefcase. Inside was her own laptop computer, as well as hard copies of the paperwork she had typed for Grace. Much too aware that Erik was watching her, she took out the first thing she saw. Praying that this was what she'd been asked for, she said, "Here is a copy of the venture proposal. But if you like, I can get—"

Erik held out his hand. "We'll start with that."

The venture proposal that Grace had prepared included the purpose and objective of the proposed business, the financing needed and the marketing strategies she had devised. It also contained detailed descriptions of the products and services she intended to offer, plus suggestions for principal suppliers and customers, as well as any other problems she anticipated. Grace had made it look so simple, Rita thought, but she knew that a lot of work and many hours had gone into formulating the proposal. It had taken a while for her just to type the thing.

Even so, she'd been fascinated. In her previous capacity as a buyer for both Glencannon's and Maxwell and Company, she'd been familiar with insurance needs, balance sheets and operating statements. But she'd never been involved in developing a master plan, or calculating things like initial capital, repayment schedules or capitalization. She was eager for the chance to learn it all.

Erik was still waiting for her to hand him the proposal. As she held it out, she caught the appraising look he gave her and wondered what he was thinking. Apparently, she'd never know, for he just smiled to himself and began to read the pages she'd given him.

Her face a blank—she hoped—she sat back and reached for her tea again. It was unnerving to feel so overwhelmed by a man she had put out of her thoughts—out of her life—months ago, and she didn't like it. What was even more disturbing was the realization that Erik seemed barely to care that she was in the room. Didn't her presence have any effect on him at all?

It seemed not, for he read through the proposal, then sat back and looked at Grace. "Interesting," he said.

Rita knew her employer could take care of herself, but she was irked by the comment. Was that all he had to say?

Grace didn't seem offended. "I know the scheme is possible," she said. "But what I want to know from you is if it's feasible?"

Erik shrugged. "By itself, the money wouldn't be much of a problem. But I imagine there will be...other factors."

Other factors? Rita thought. *What other factors?* She couldn't imagine that Grace had forgotten anything.

Grace knew what he was referring to. "You mean the DeWilde Corporation," she said. "You think they'll fight me on this."

Erik looked down at the folder he'd put in his lap. He seemed to be debating about something, for when he looked up, he said, "May I be honest?"

If you are, it will be the first time, Rita thought. But this was Grace's show, so she held her tongue. She was here to observe and to take notes, and to learn everything she could. She wasn't here to start a fight or try to influence Grace not to trust this man. That, she decided, could wait until they left.

"I expect your honesty, Erik," Grace said. "That's why I'm here."

"Before we go on, I need to ask you a few personal questions."

"Ask away," Grace said. "I can't promise I'll be able to answer them all."

"These you will be," Erik assured her. "It's no secret that you and your husband have...separated. Or that you own a block of the DeWilde Corporation stock. I'm sure you realize that the business world—not to mention the financial community—is anxiously waiting to see what develops."

"What you really mean is that everyone is curious about whether or not I intend to sell."

"It is a legitimate concern."

"I agree. I haven't decided yet."

"I gathered that. Otherwise, you wouldn't be here talking to me."

"That's true." Grace paused. "You told me you'd be honest, Erik, so I intend to be, as well. The truth is, my situation is in such a state of flux right now that I'd rather use the sale of the stock as a last resort. If I can initiate this store on my own, I'd much prefer that."

"I understand. But opening a store could cause problems in itself. I'm sure you'll agree that the De-Wilde Corporation has a vested interest in protecting its name, not to mention guarding that particular area of competition."

"DeWilde's does not have a monopoly on bridal departments."

Erik smiled. "I'd hardly call a DeWilde store a bridal *department*."

Grace had to smile, too. "Point well taken. I'm aware of that, more so than anyone, since I helped to develop the concept."

"You're being modest. It's well known that you helped to cultivate the DeWilde philosophy and have been the driving force behind its marketing strategy."

"You flatter me, Erik," Grace insisted.

"I don't think so. But I do feel it's safe to say that your departure has caused some alarm at corporation headquarters."

"You seem remarkably well-informed about the DeWildes."

"It's my job," Erik said. "But I have to admit, it's been difficult finding information. For a family who owns and operates a company that size, there's been remarkably little adverse publicity."

"It's a private family, I agree. They were not happy when I decided to...defect."

Rita heard the bitter note Grace couldn't hide. Her new employer hadn't shared the intimate details of her crumbling marriage with her, and Rita didn't expect her to. But she still felt sad about it. After all, Grace and Jeffrey had been married a long time. Their separation had to be a painful experience for Grace, and even though Rita had known her for such a short time, she wished she could help.

Erik had heard the painful undertone to Grace's voice, too. "I don't mean to cause you distress, but if we're to go forward on this, we all have to develop a clear view of the situation. And at this point, I think it's probably safe to say that your intention to open a store—under any guise, under any name—is going to be contested by the DeWildes."

"You're probably right," Grace agreed. "But it's not going to deter me."

Erik smiled. "Good. Then we understand each other."

"We do, indeed," Grace said. She stood. "And now, I believe we have taken enough of your time."

Erik stood with her, as did Rita. "Before you go," he said, "I'd like you to meet my partner, Rudy Laughton. As a lawyer, he'll be handling whatever legal aspects come up. If you have time, Eleanor can take you to his office. It's just down the hall."

"I'd like that." Grace held out her hand. "I'll be in touch."

He shook her hand. "It's been a pleasure."

Grace started out, Rita behind her. But before they got to the door, Erik said, "Could I talk to you for a minute, Rita?"

Stiffly, Rita turned to him. "Oh, I don't think—"

To her dismay, Grace said, "It's all right. I'll meet you here after I talk to Mr. Laughton."

Left with no choice, Rita watched as Erik's secretary appeared and led Grace away. The last thing she wanted was to be alone with this man, so before he could say anything, she took refuge in business details. Opening her briefcase again, she began, "We have additional information for you. Executive summaries, business descriptions, projections—"

She was searching for the documents when Erik put his hand over hers. Quietly, he said, "I'll look at them later. Right now, I'd like to know...how have you been?"

He shouldn't have touched her, she thought with a pang. She would have been all right if he'd just kept his distance—or if Grace had still been in the room with them. But they were alone now, and the moment she felt his fingers on hers, the fragile control she'd been maintaining began to crumble. She took her hand away.

"How have I *been?*" she repeated. She tried to be cool and sophisticated, but in spite of herself her dark eyes flashed. "Now, that's an interesting question coming from you."

He winced, but his gaze held hers. "I told you at the time that I was sorry."

"Yes, so you did. And as you might recall, *I* told *you* that wasn't good enough. I haven't changed my mind."

"I apologized. What more can I do?"

She stared at him incredulously. "You really are unbelievable. It's clear that you're still the same arrogant, detestable man you always were. It doesn't matter that you betrayed me and every other Glencannon employee. And for what? So you could prove how smart you were? So you could make more money?"

He looked uncomfortable. "It wasn't like that."

"Wasn't it? People's *lives* were ruined, Erik. If you could have seen Mr. Glencannon that last day—"

She couldn't talk about it anymore or she'd say something she was sure she'd regret. Abruptly, she moved away. Trying to control herself, she went to the window and stared blindly out at the skyline. She knew she had to get a grip on herself before Grace came back.

"I am sorry, Rita," Erik said behind her. "I'd like to make it up to you, if I can."

"Why?" she asked, without turning around. Before he could answer, she gestured angrily with her hand. "Never mind, it doesn't matter anymore. It's over."

"If you feel that way, why are you still so upset?"

"I'm not upset!"

"You could have fooled me."

She did turn around at that, intending to fling some scathing remark at him about how *she'd* been the one who'd been fooled. But she hadn't expected him to be standing so close to her. When she realized he was only a step or so away, she jerked backward. He reached out a hand to steady her.

"Don't touch me!" she warned, when she felt his fingers on her arm.

He didn't let go. She tried to pull away, but he held on firmly, and when she made the mistake of glancing up at his face, she ceased her struggles. For a tense moment or two, they just stood there, staring into each other's eyes.

Try as she might, Rita couldn't control what was happening to her. The desire that he'd always been able to evoke flashed through her with a jolt, and against her will she felt herself being drawn toward him. For a wild moment, she wanted to put her arms around his neck and pull his head down to hers. Almost without realizing it, she parted her lips, and her eyes began to drift closed. Oh, to kiss him again, to feel his arms around her, to know the sensation of his body against hers!

Reason returned and she pulled back. "Please, let go of me," she said coldly.

This time, he obliged. But as she walked toward the door, she knew his eyes were following her. She wanted to tell him that she hated him, but the words wouldn't come. They both waited in tense silence until Grace returned. She was accompanied by Erik's partner, Rudy Laughton. During the introductions and small talk that briefly followed, Rita was able to edge away from Erik. When they finally left, she breathed a sigh of relief. She'd never been so glad to escape from a place in her life.

RITA WAS HARDLY surprised when Grace turned to her in the cab and said, "I didn't realize that you and Erik already knew each other."

This was her opening; she had to take it. "If I'd known he was the man we were going to see, I would have warned you."

Grace looked taken aback. "Warned me?"

"Yes. Erik Mulholland is not a nice man."

"You mean personally?"

Rita's voice hardened. "I mean in every way."

"I take it you're referring to his reputation as a corporate raider."

"It's a reputation that's well justified, believe me. Remember that hostile takeover of Glencannon's that I mentioned? He was responsible for that."

Grace was silent a moment. Then she said, "He comes very highly recommended."

"I'm sure he does. He's very good at his job."

"Yes, that's why I wanted to talk to him." Grace tapped a finger to her lips, pondering. "This puts a different spin on things, doesn't it?"

Rita was almost afraid to ask. "What do you mean?"

"Well, I have to admit I was impressed with him. But if I decide to work with him, I suspect that might make things difficult where you're concerned, won't it?"

Rita wanted to groan. Had she been as transparent as that? But of course she had; everyone who knew her kidded her constantly about what a terrible liar she'd make. However, she wasn't prepared to answer Grace's question until she'd had a chance to think about it.

Cautiously, she asked, "Have you decided to work with him?"

To her relief, Grace said, "No, I haven't." Her relief was short-lived, though, as Grace added, "But I have to say I'm inclined toward the idea. I also liked his partner. I think they make a good team.''

Without warning, an image flashed through Rita's mind. It was one of Erik's powerful, lean body suspended over hers. She could see the sheen of sweat glistening on the muscles of his arms as he lowered himself down on her; she could feel the weight of his body. She closed her eyes. Once, she thought, they had made a good team, too.

Fiercely, she thrust both the image and the thought away. That affair was in the past; what she had to deal with now was the unpleasant present.

Fortunately for her, the cab pulled up at the apartment building just then, and she was saved from having to make a reply.

As Grace headed inside, she turned to Rita with a smile. "You've put in a full day, Rita. Go home and relax. We can talk about Eric Mulholland in the morning."

Rita certainly didn't offer any objections. With a wave goodbye, she headed toward her car. A reprieve, however brief, was what she needed right now. Time to sort out the emotions warring inside her; time to think rationally about what course of action to take. Time to prepare herself—personally and professionally—to deal with Eric again.

BECAUSE OF A TRAFFIC accident, it took Rita more than an hour to drive home. Far too much time, she decided, for her to be sitting in a car thinking about Erik.

She had a real problem now, she mused, as four endless lines of traffic moved forward, six inches at a time. What was she going to do about it? Could she work with Erik Mulholland?

She closed her eyes. Without effort, she could feel his lips on hers, and remember how that contact had transported her instantly to another dimension. She recalled the texture of his hair, the scent of his skin, the gaze that seemed to pierce her very soul....

Someone honked his horn impatiently, and with a start, she came back to the present. She realized that she was trembling; her hand on the wheel shook as if she had palsy. If just the memory of him could do this to her, how could she even think of trying to work with the flesh-and-blood man?

She couldn't do it, she thought. She'd have to tell Grace tomorrow that she'd thought about it, but it was impossible. If Grace hired Erik Mulholland, then she'd just have to quit.

Quit? And walk away from an opportunity like this? Was she crazy? How could she even think such a thought?

Erik's face appeared in her mind once more, but this time his expression taunted her. He seemed to be saying that she would never get ahead if she couldn't set personal feelings aside for a professional goal.

And he was right, she thought in sudden anger. What was the matter with her? She'd dreamed of a chance like this for years. Now that it was within her grasp, was she just going to walk away?

No, she decided, and resolved that when she got to work the next morning, the first thing she'd tell her employer was that if Grace hired Erik, she'd have no problem working with him.

After all, she thought, as traffic finally opened up and she was able to get across the bridge to Sausalito, where she lived, she and Erik were professionals. As long as she kept everything on a strictly business level, there wouldn't be any problem.

No problem at all.

CHAPTER FOUR

THE SHANNON FAMILY was a large one. Rita was one of five sisters and two brothers, and as the oldest girl, she'd been like a second mother to her younger siblings. But she had always been closest to her sister Marie, who was two years younger than she. On Saturday afternoon, Rita was cleaning house when Marie called. As always, her sister dispensed with pleasantries and got right to the point.

"So," Marie said, "how's the job going?"

Rita had been so excited about working with Grace that she had immediately told everyone in the family about her new position. Gladly setting aside the mop she'd been using on the kitchen floor, she threw herself into a chair and said, "It's going just fine."

"You're working for a woman you've admired ever since college days, and all you can say is that it's going *fine*?"

Rita grinned. "I was trying to be cool and sophisticated, but I should have known that you'd see right through me. All right, it's great. It's only been a week, but I'm learning something every day. The woman is fascinating."

"So, when is the new store going to open?"

Rita laughed. "Not for a while. These things take time. We're still working on the concept. In fact, we haven't even started to scout locations. But I have contacted a real estate agent who's poring over available space."

"I can't wait," Marie said with a sigh. "I've always wanted to visit a DeWilde store."

"So have I. But this isn't another DeWilde's. It's going to be different."

"How so?"

"Well, we're going to make it more...San Francisco. In fact—and don't tell anyone yet, because it's just an idea—we've been thinking that maybe a dynamite store opening would feature a black wedding gown, with all-white for the attendants."

Marie whistled. "That's a little avant-garde even for this city, don't you think?"

"No, I think it's a fabulous idea. And it will certainly get attention."

"That it will. The problem is, what will you do for an encore?"

"Oh, I'll think of something."

"That sounds just like you. You've always been so confident."

An image of Erik flashed into her mind, and Rita winced. At Grace's request, she had run some additional papers over to Erik's office yesterday on her lunch hour. She had hoped he'd be out at that time, but he hadn't been, and when he had asked her to lunch, she'd been so shocked she couldn't think of a refusal. They'd gone to a new place in town near his office, and they'd barely been seated before she was wondering how much she'd regret it if she just jumped up and ran out before they ordered. Why had she accepted his invitation? She didn't want to have lunch with this man; she wanted to see as little of him as possible.

But there they were, and after she'd forced herself to order a salad she didn't want and knew she'd never be able to eat, he disconcerted her even more by being as charming as possible. Or maybe, she thought, it was the big glass of wine she'd had before her salad came. She'd gulped it down as if it were an elixir, and after that, she wasn't so nervous anymore.

Erik had asked her how she liked her new job, too. And she had told him, as she'd just told Marie, that she loved every minute of it so far.

"I can understand why," he'd said. "Grace De-Wilde is a remarkable woman."

Rita had nodded in agreement. Talking about Grace seemed safe enough. "She certainly is. I know that when the new store opens, it's going to take off like a rocket. You can't believe the wonderful ideas she has—" She stopped when she saw his face. "What's wrong?"

"Oh, nothing—yet. But I think there might be a few problems ahead."

"Yes, Grace mentioned that she had talked to you about the fuss her husband is kicking up over the new store. She didn't seem particularly worried about it, though." She paused. "Should she be?"

"No, it's nothing that Rudy and I can't handle...for now, anyway. And we anticipated that the corporation wouldn't like it that Grace was edging into their territory."

"It's not their territory!" she'd said fiercely. "Grace has every right to open up a business anywhere she wants!"

"Yes, but this isn't just any business. And she might not have the right to call it DeWilde's."

Rita calmed down. "She knows that. And it doesn't matter. She's leaning toward calling it 'Grace,' anyway."

"I like that," he'd said. "It has a simple elegance to it, just like the woman herself."

Rita had agreed with that, too. "She is elegant, isn't she? I wish I was just half as smart and savvy as she is."

"You have your good qualities, too."

The wine made her brash—or foolish. "Oh, do you think so?" she'd asked.

And just like that, the atmosphere had become charged. His expression changed, and he leaned forward, his eyes holding hers. "You know I do."

She didn't know what to say. There were two roads here, and she didn't want to go down either of them, so she looked away, spied her almost-empty wineglass and grabbed it. All that was left was a drop or two, but she drank it, anyway. Mercifully, the waiter came with their orders. When he left, she was so determined to steer clear of personal remarks that she babbled about anything that came into her head. In fact, she talked so fast that Erik couldn't have gotten a word in edgewise if he'd tried.

And he didn't—at least not until lunch was over. They were out on the street again, about to go their separate ways, when he said, "I enjoyed that, Rita. We'll have to do it again."

She knew this wasn't what he meant, but she said, "I imagine we'll have more business meetings now that we're both going to be working for Grace." She didn't give him a chance to reply. For once, a taxi was parked nearby and she jumped into it, quickly waving goodbye.

"SO, ANYWAY, Colleen and I agreed last night that the best thing you ever did was quit Maxwell and Company. It took you long enough, don't you think? Rita? Rita, are you listening to me?"

Rita came out of her reverie. "Of course I am," she said, although she hadn't heard a word for the past five minutes. "What were you saying?"

Marie sighed. "I was saying that I never did understand why you didn't leave your job at Maxwell long before. You and your misguided loyalty! You could have gone to any other store and worked your way up to head buyer again in nothing flat."

"Yes, but if I had, I wouldn't have been looking for a job at the time Grace came to San Francisco and needed an assistant. So it all worked out perfectly."

"That's true. So I guess it wasn't a sign that it was time for you to think about settling down, after all."

"Settle down?" Rita shuddered. "I've told you all a thousand times I never want to get married."

"You might change your mind. And if you wait too long—"

"Oh, please—spare me the ticking biological clock. You know what I think about that. It was concocted by white male Republicans who are determined to keep women in their place. Besides, after what I've seen you and Colleen and Martha and Louise go through with your kids, not to mention the problems Terry and Jim have had, why would I want a spouse and kids of my own?"

"You don't mean that."

"Yes, I do," Rita said stubbornly. "But let's not argue about it. I'm sure that marriage and children are two of the greatest joys in life. In fact, I'm even willing to concede that they are. But haven't we forgotten one thing?''

"And what's that?"

"Maybe before I start rhapsodizing about getting married and having children, I should first have a candidate for husband and father in my life. Or at least on the horizon.''

"Maybe you would have had someone in your life before now if your standards weren't so impossibly high.''

"I'm just particular.''

"You're impossible.''

"Maybe he's not even out there.''

"How do you know if you won't even *look*?''

"I thought we weren't going to argue about this.''

"We're not. I called to ask you something else, anyway. You were supposed to find a place where we could have Mom and Dad's anniversary party. Have you done that yet?''

Rita groaned. With too many other things on her mind, she had forgotten all about it. Guiltily, she said, "I'll do it right away.''

"Oh, Reetz! It's not every day our parents celebrate their thirty-fifth wedding anniversary! I want this to be right.''

"I know, I know. Don't worry, I'll take care of it.''

"I hope so.''

"I *will*, I promise.''

After Rita hung up the phone, she took a cup of coffee and went outside. She had moved to Sausalito some time ago, and the back deck of the house she was renting looked out over the bay. It was a peaceful scene, but she felt anything but calm as she sat down and stared out at the water.

The last few days had been as unsettling for her employer as they had been for her. Grace had received a silver basket filled with a bottle of champagne and Italian candied almonds—accompanied by an announcement that her son, Gabriel, and his fiancée, Lianne Beecham, had eloped. Rita knew with how much pleasure Grace had anticipated helping Gabe and Lianne plan their wedding; it was her specialty, after all. Furthermore, it might have provided the perfect opportunity for her to mend her relationship with her son, which had become estranged ever since she'd left her husband and family and moved to San Francisco. Grace hadn't seemed her usual energetic self on Friday, and Rita was sure that her lack of enthusiasm and drive was due in part, at least, to the shock of the announcement.

Rita couldn't help but be affected by Grace's mood, though she recognized that her own inner turmoil had a different source. Now that Grace had officially enlisted Erik to find investors for her new store, Rita had to come to terms with the fact that he was going to be part of her professional future.

She had managed to weather meeting Erik again after so long without making too much of a fool of herself—yet. But since they were going to be working together, she had to get her feelings under control. Still, just thinking about it made her impatient. Why was she dwelling on *feelings* when her entire future was at stake? She'd always prided herself on her professionalism, and she was going to be good at this job. She knew it; she could feel it. She wasn't going to blow this opportunity, because it wouldn't come again.

The portable phone she'd brought out with her rang, making her jump. Sure that it was her sister calling back, she picked it up and said, "What is it now, Marie?"

There was a short silence, then Erik said, "Sorry to disappoint you, but this is—"

She knew who it was. The instant she heard his voice, her traitorous heart started to pound, and she sat up straight. "I know who it is. Hello, Erik. How did you get this number?"

"Grace gave it to me when I called her this morning. I'm sorry to bother you, especially on a weekend."

"No problem," she said, remembering her vow to be businesslike. "What can I help you with?"

"I was going to talk to Grace about a few questions on the material you left yesterday, but she wasn't feeling well, so she suggested I call you. Do you have a minute?"

"Sure," she said, proud of herself for sounding so casual when her pulse was leaping around like a frog. "What questions do you have?"

He hesitated. "It would be easier if we could do this face-to-face. I promise, it won't take long."

At the suggestion that they meet, she tensed again. Trying to think of an excuse, she asked, "Without Grace?"

"As I mentioned, she's not feeling well. And I really would like to go over some of this material so I can determine exactly what her needs are."

Rita didn't want to meet him alone again, without the leavening, comforting, *refereeing* presence of her employer. Trying to think, she said, "I'm not sure I can help you, Erik. Grace is the one who—"

"She said that you'd know what I needed at this point. I really hate to press you on this, Rita, but Grace wants to get the ball rolling."

Rita knew that was true. When she thought about how it would look to her employer if she refused this simple request, she said reluctantly, "All right. Where would you like to meet, and when?"

"Obviously, with Grace not feeling well, we can't meet at her apartment. How about my office?"

She would have preferred a location that wasn't so much his turf, but as he'd pointed out, they couldn't go to the apartment. Thinking that she was going to have to find them a proper office, and soon, she said, "All right. Are you there now? If so, I can meet you in about an hour."

When she hung up the phone, she had to clasp her hands together to stop them from shaking. "You can do this," she told herself. "You know you can."

An hour later, dressed in a business suit, she arrived at Erik's office. Even though it was the weekend, she had hoped that his secretary would be there. But Eleanor's desk was empty, the machines silent and covered, the blotter clean and orderly. Erik's door was open; he heard her come in, for he immediately appeared on the threshold.

"Thanks for coming," he said with a cautious smile.

She smiled tightly, too. Already she felt uncomfortable, for in contrast to her business attire, he was dressed casually in slacks and a sports shirt. "It wasn't a problem. I was glad to do it for Grace."

Having established that she was here only for her employer's benefit, she walked by him into his office. When she saw papers spread out on the coffee table instead of the desk, she headed in that direction. But instead of taking a seat on the sofa, she chose one of the chairs and sat, her briefcase firmly on her lap.

"Now," she said briskly, "what can I help you with?"

He followed her to the conference area—but not before she caught his amused smile at her businesslike tone. At least she hoped it was her tone. She bristled at the idea that he might be laughing at her.

But he was all seriousness as he sat down on the sofa and began to speak. "Before we get into specific questions, I'd like you to give me another general overview of the plans for the new store."

She frowned. "You have the figures—"

"I know. But as I'm sure you're well aware, there are many causes of business failures in retail trade. Economic, sales, expenses . . ."

"I could appreciate your apprehension if you were talking about an inexperienced entrepreneur, Erik, but this is Grace DeWilde."

"I understand that. But with the high rate of retail attrition, we have to be concerned about any obstacles the DeWilde Corporation might erect to block her enterprise."

"If so, that's a conversation you should have with Grace herself, not me."

"I will. I only mentioned it because we were talking about issues that contribute to business failures."

She did bristle at that. "Surely you don't think that Grace DeWilde will fail!"

"I don't think so, but others might be more skeptical. You'd have to agree that the DeWilde Corporation casts a long shadow in the retail world."

"But that's exactly why Grace has come to you and Rudy. She wants to distance herself as much as she can from the corporation."

"That might be difficult to do."

"Why?"

"Because she was an officer of that corporation. And as I mentioned before, it's no secret what her contribution was to the company."

"What difference does that make? She won't be using the DeWilde name."

"I'm not sure that's going to matter to the money people. But we'll see. In the meantime, why don't you tell me something about the actual plans for the store."

"Do you mean the proposed layout?"

"That, or anything else you want to tell me."

"Well, you know that we haven't determined a location for the store yet. But no matter where we finally open, we'll have to allocate space for specific activities like storage, selling, workrooms, displays, receiving sections—"

"Rita," Erik said.

"What?"

"You're not going to make it easy for me, are you?"

"I don't know what you mean."

He leaned forward. Although they were sitting some distance apart, she couldn't help but move slightly back. Her instinctive gesture of retreat irritated her even more. "Erik, I—"

"We have to talk about it, Rita. If we don't, it will be like a giant wall between us, and will probably affect not only our work for Grace, but also our own relationship."

"What relationship?"

"The one we have while we're working for a woman we much admire. I want to do right by her. Don't you?"

"How can you ask that? Of course I do."

"Then why don't we get it over with? Get it out in the open, have a fight about it—or whatever we're going to do—and move on?"

She didn't want to talk about this, not when she'd spent so much time convincing herself that she would work with him—and to hell with the past. "If you're referring to what happened last year, I've forgotten all about it."

It was a stupid thing to say, and she knew it the instant the words were out of her mouth. So did he, because he asked, "If you've forgotten it, how did you know what I was talking about?"

"Look," she said, trying to recover both her poise and her wits, "it doesn't matter anymore. As you told me so vehemently at the time, it was business. In fact, I believe your exact words were that you were just doing your job."

"I'm not talking about what happened with Glencannon's, Rita. I'm talking about what happened between us."

"I doubt now that there ever was an 'us,' Erik. Now, please, can we get back to the business at hand? Discussing a trivial affair seems to be a waste of time."

He stared at her a moment longer, then he sighed. "Maybe you're right. I seem to have attributed more importance to it than it actually had. Now, where were we?"

Where they were, Rita thought, was exactly nowhere. Wondering why she felt so unsettled and dissatisfied and angry when she had won her point, she made herself carry on a discussion about marketing and kinds of merchandise, projected size of the inventory and the like. But the entire time she was saying all the right things, and giving Erik all the correct facts and figures, she knew she should have said what was on her mind. Maybe, as he had indicated, if they'd had a knock-down, drag-out fight about it, they could put the past behind them. If nothing else, it would have cleared the air, and it certainly would have made her feel better, she thought glumly.

But she'd missed her chance, and she couldn't back-track now. She had insisted that their blistering affair had been a mere blip on the radar screen of relation-ships, and if she indicated that she wanted to discuss it after all, it would be obvious that she'd been lying through her teeth.

She managed to get through the meeting. When they were finished, she busied herself with packing up the additional papers she'd brought so she wouldn't have to look at him. "I'll write up a memo of the things we discussed today for Grace. I'm sure she'll have ques-tions and additional input. In fact, she'll probably want to see you herself."

He walked her to the door. "I'll be glad to meet her any time except Monday. I have people coming in from Belgium and I have to meet with them."

"Fine. I'll tell her."

Until that point, she believed she was going to es-cape without incident. But as she started out, Erik put a hand on her arm and stopped her. "Wait—"

Even through her sleeve, she could feel the warmth of his fingers. It kindled memories of the sensation his hands had once elicited in her, and she briefly closed her eyes before she looked up at him.

"What is it?" she asked.

He gazed down at her, those damned blue eyes of his so intense and oh so sincere. Softly, he said, "I know you won't believe me, but I really am sorry for what happened, Rita. And since we're going to be working together, I'd like for us to be friends.''

Friends? After they'd been lovers? Fat chance, she thought. She moved away, pretending to adjust her purse strap. "That's fine with me. As I told you, it's all in the past.''

"In that case," he said, holding her gaze, "would you have dinner with me?''

First it was lunch. Now it was dinner. What would it be after that? She knew she should make some excuse, but for the life of her, she couldn't think of one.

"Erik, I—''

"We'll take the ferry to Larkspur and have dinner at a restaurant there. We always said we'd do that, remember?''

She didn't want to remember. She didn't want to think of things they'd said they would do and had never done. But it was the end of June, a time of beautiful sunsets, and what could she say to that?

THEY TOOK THE FERRY to Larkspur and had dinner at a tiny place called Destime's. They were careful to talk of inconsequential things; not once did they refer to the fact that they'd been lovers. But all through a meal she never tasted, Rita was aware of Erik's dark blue gaze, for every time she looked up, his eyes were on her face.

She watched his hands as he ate and drank, and tried not to think how his touch had once set her ablaze; she stared at his mouth while he was talking, and felt a monumental ache gnawing inside her. But somehow she managed not to mention the past, and because she avoided it, so did he. They both pretended the only reason they were there at all was because of Grace, but long before the meal was over, Rita knew that this had been a mistake. She shouldn't have come, and now it was too late.

Darkness had fallen by the time they took the ferry back to the city. But it was one of those rare perfect nights in San Francisco when the fog hovered far enough offshore so that the stars could shine through. The water flowing under the boat was calm, the gentle breeze like a caress. The famous Golden Gate Bridge seemed suspended in space; it glowed like a delicate spider web, festooned with golden lace.

She and Erik went out on deck, and as they stood side by side, Rita was so achingly aware of him that her knees felt weak. She had to say something to break this growing spell, so finally, after a long silence, she said, "I enjoyed myself tonight, Erik. I'm glad we came."

He turned to look at her, and in the lights from the wheelhouse, his eyes were almost black. "So am I," he said huskily, and almost without volition, it seemed, he ran his fingers gently down her cheek.

She couldn't help herself. The tender caress was her undoing, and before she realized it, she was reaching up to take his hand in hers.

The ferry docked.

The spell that had woven around them dissolved with that gentle bump against the landing, and much later, when she couldn't sleep, Rita tried to tell herself she was glad it had happened when it had. Who knew what she would have said or done if they hadn't been interrupted?

But she knew it would be a long, long time, if ever, before she forgot how Erik had touched her that night. That simple gesture had been both tender and erotic, but what was even more significant was the fact that never, not even during the height of their passionate love affair, had he ever touched her in quite that way.

What did it mean? She wasn't sure. She just knew that if he ever touched her like that again, she might not care what happened after.

CHAPTER FIVE

FOR THE NEXT couple of weeks, Rita and Grace went all over San Francisco looking for the right location for the new store. They were both discouraged when they returned to the apartment at the end of another long afternoon, and with a tired sigh, Grace sank down on the couch.

"I'm beginning to think this quest will *never* end," she said. "One would think there would be numerous prospects in a city this size, yet nothing seems right."

Rita had tried to be optimistic, but she was just as weary as Grace. Everything they'd looked at so far had either been too cramped, too dark, too gloomy, too old or—in the case of a building that had once been a health club facility—too big and drafty.

Still, when she saw how fatigued Grace looked, she said encouragingly, "We'll find something. I'm sure we haven't exhausted all the possibilities."

"I know we will—eventually. I suppose that, what with everything else that has been going on, I was foolish to expect that the search for store space would be easy."

"You've just been trying to do too much," Rita assured her. "Not only have we been scouting store locations, but you've been trying to find more furniture for your apartment. And, don't forget, you've also been putting a lot of time into arranging a reception for your son and his new wife."

"Yes, but I want to do that," Grace said. She sighed again. "I feel so guilty about leaving without giving poor Lianne any indication of what was happening. The poor girl showed up for her new job, only to discover that the person who had hired her had left the company. At the time, I wasn't thinking. I just wanted to get away."

"That's understandable."

"But now, when I'm trying to make it up to both her and Gabriel, Jeffrey and I can't agree on any detail about the reception, not even the date and time. It's already mid-July. Sometimes I think I should just let it go."

"Oh, but you don't want to do that, do you? You were looking forward to it so much."

"I know. After missing the wedding itself, I wanted to do this one special thing. But this planning—or lack thereof—is getting out of hand." Grace gestured with frustration. "I just can't do a thing from here. If I was in England, maybe it would be different."

"Maybe Michael Forrest can help," Rita suggested. "From what you've said about him, he's quite adept at social occasions. And doesn't he plan to travel to London in the near future? Perhaps he can act as a . . . liaison."

Grace smiled at the mention of Michael Forrest. In her tangled Powell family tree, his mother was her first cousin. When he had inherited a major holding in his family's Carlisle Forrest Hotels, he had immediately thrown the entire chain into chaos by seeking to transform the once exclusive and elegant hotels into glitzy Hollywood versions. Everyone else had been horrified, but Grace was amused. Michael had always been seduced by the glamour of showbiz, but he was bright and energetic, and Grace thought he had vision. Whether it was the right vision or not remained to be seen.

Michael had called recently to extend his condolences about her separation from Jeffrey, and to offer any help she might need. She intended to take him up on his offer when they began planning the grand opening for the store.

"Ah, yes," she said affectionately. "Michael of the peripatetic life-style. No one can throw a party like him. The only problem is that he travels so much that no one ever knows where he is. I'm not sure he'd be able to help with the reception for Gabe and Lianne. Still, one of his hotels is here in San Francisco, and he has promised to stop by soon. Assuming we ever get to the stage of planning an opening for the store, I'll definitely consult him." She smiled again before going on. "If he's involved, the only problem will be getting him to tone it down. Michael *does* have a tendency to go over the top. And perhaps I can get my niece Mallory to cater it."

"Mallory?"

"My brother Leland's daughter. She owns Mallory's near Union Square."

"Well that should certainly take care of things nicely!"

"Yes, it should. And now I think we should call it a day."

"I agree," Rita said. She glanced around the living room cum office. "I'll stay awhile and straighten up in here."

If Grace hadn't been fighting the summer cold she'd caught, she probably would have argued. "I'll only accept if you promise to go home yourself after that. I don't want to wear you out."

Rita laughed. "No danger of that. I love it all. You couldn't drive me away with a stick."

Grace sighed as she got up. "This hasn't gone at all the way I planned."

"You're just not feeling well. Tomorrow you'll feel better and be able to tackle the world again."

"I hope you're right. Well, good night, or I guess I should say, good afternoon."

After Grace had disappeared into the master bedroom and shut the door, Rita busied herself for a while with paperwork. She was just debating about taking off early when the phone rang. Before it could sound again and disturb Grace, she reached for it and whispered a hello.

"Rita?" a familiar voice said.

"Oh . . . Erik," she said.

He heard her hesitation. "Is this a bad time?"

She kept her voice down. "I'm afraid so. Grace wasn't feeling well, so she's resting. Can I take a message?"

"Well . . . this is difficult. Have you found a location for the store yet?"

"No, why?"

"Because I got a line on a place just now that I think might be what she's looking for. The real estate agent is a friend of mine, and I asked her to keep it to herself until I talked to Grace about it. It's in a prime location, and you know how fast those go once they're on the market."

After her experiences during the past couple of weeks, Rita knew all too well. She glanced toward the bedroom, then said reluctantly, "I hate to do it, but if there's a rush, I suppose I can disturb her."

"Well, you know what she wants, don't you? We could check it out and report back to her."

"I don't know, Erik. I wouldn't want to make a decision on something so important by myself."

"You wouldn't have to sign anything," he said persuasively. "All you'd have to do is tell me if you think Grace would be interested."

Rita considered. She didn't want to drag Grace off to yet another disappointment when she wasn't feeling well, and wasn't this type of thing just what executive assistants were for? As Erik had said, they were just going to look. The final decision still rested with Grace.

"All right," she said. "I guess I could go."

When Erik picked her up in front of the apartment building five minutes later, he had to tap the horn for her to recognize him. When they'd gone to dinner at Larkspur, they'd taken the trolley. Today, he was driving a sleek black Jaguar. As she quickly got in and slammed the car door to a chorus of irritated motorists sounding off at the minuscule delay, she said breathlessly, "Nice car. When did you get this?"

"Last year," he said, swinging smoothly back into heavy traffic. "It was easier ferrying clients around in this rather than trying to fit them into the other car."

The other car had been a gold Porsche. When she remembered how they had laughed about the gearshift console being in the way at significant moments, she said hastily, "I can see why." She looked out the window. "Where is this place?"

"Near Kearny and Post."

Since that location was in the heart of the city's shopping center, she looked at him in amazement. "But we've been all over that area with the proverbial fine-tooth comb and haven't found a thing!''

He took his eyes off the street long enough to give her a smile. ''I told you, this just came up. I wouldn't have known about it, either, if I didn't have a friend in the business. When Grace told me about the problems that you were having finding the right location, I put the word out that I was looking for store space.''

''I see.''

''You don't sound pleased.''

''No, I am,'' she insisted, although to her annoyance, she was a little jealous. She'd been turning over rocks in an effort to find the right place; Erik had made a phone call or two. It didn't seem fair. ''It's just that we've been searching day and night and haven't found anything suitable. Grace is beginning to believe space is not only at a premium, it's impossible to find. I have to say I agree with her.''

Erik pulled into a parking place. ''Maybe this will be the one. Here we are.''

While he got out and came around to open her door, Rita had time to scrutinize the outside of the building. It had a dingy stone facade and cracked leaded windows, but despite its disreputable appearance, she felt a stirring of excitement. Erik was right, she thought. This could be the place!

She and Grace had been looking for something different, something sophisticated and elegant, yet with an old-world appearance. As Rita stared at the building, her vivid imagination helped her to picture how it would look when the stone facade was sandblasted clean and the windows replaced. In her vision, she could almost see a small but refined sign outside: Grace.

Trying not to let her enthusiasm get the best of her, she got out of the car. Erik had the key, and she waited impatiently while he fiddled with the stubborn lock. Already making mental notes—this one about having the lock replaced—she eagerly proceeded him into the store.

The interior was dusty and dim, with very little light filtering in through the smeared windows at the front. The previous tenant seemed to have left in a hurry, for a battered display case stood on end near the door, and a jumble of cardboard boxes created a maze that they had to push aside before they could go any farther. A light fixture dangled from a fraying cord overhead, but when Erik tried the switch, nothing happened.

"I didn't realize the electricity would be off," he said. "I guess we should have brought flashlights."

His voice echoed in the big empty space, and as Rita peered into the gloom toward the back of the store, she agreed. "That, or miners' hats."

"Well, this is useless. Since we can't see our hands in front of our faces, we might as well—wait a minute. Where are you going?"

Rita wasn't going to let the lack of a little light stop her from investigating. This was the most promising store space she had seen yet, and she couldn't go without exploring every inch. Already, ideas were bubbling over in her head; in her mind's eye, she could see what a contrast a little fresh paint and some wall-to-wall carpet could make. This large front space could be utilized as a display area, she thought. They could pose a few mannequins around, and over there they could put—

"Watch out!"

She'd been so involved in imagining how many changes they could make that she hadn't been watching where she was going. Erik's warning shout startled her as she was stepping onto a raised platform, and she turned to him in surprise when he jumped forward and grabbed her elbow.

"Don't look at me like that," he warned. "I just saved you from a broken ankle."

He pointed, and when she looked down, she saw that if she'd taken one more step, she would have had a nasty tumble. The area she'd thought was a dais was just a pile of lumber stacked haphazardly on the floor. In fact, as she was balancing there, it shifted slightly with her weight, and with Erik still holding on to her, she carefully stepped off.

"Thanks," she said.

"Think nothing of it," he said wryly, letting go of her. "Now, are you ready to leave?"

"Leave? You've got to be kidding. I want to see it all."

"But you can't see anything. It's too dark in here."

"I can see enough to give a report to Grace when I'm finished."

"I think we should come back."

"No," she said stubbornly. "You can leave if you want, but I'm going to check out the entire place. Oh, look—stairs! I didn't realize there was a second floor. It will be perfect for storage and offices."

She started off, Erik close behind her. "Wait a minute," he said. "If you're so insistent on this, at least let me go first."

Without stopping, she shot him an indignant look over her shoulder. "I'm perfectly capable of exploring on my own, thank you very much. I don't need a man to run interference. Come or not, but I'm going ahead."

Suiting action to words, she went briskly up the stairs and emerged into a gloomy atticlike space above. Up here, the dimness was alleviated by a small fan-shaped window at one end of the large room; she was trying to get her bearings when Erik came up behind her. Disturbed by their feet, dust motes swirled up into what little light there was, and he sneezed.

"Well, this is promising, isn't it," he said.

Ignoring his sarcasm, Rita went forward. "As a matter of fact, it is," she said, excited all over again. "There's more than enough storage area, and look! Over there, we can put up walls or partitions or something, and have all the office space we need." She turned to him, her lips parted, her eyes—even in that faint light—sparkling. "Oh, Erik, I think Grace is really going to—"

She never got a chance to finish the sentence. Erik was facing her, when suddenly he glanced over her shoulder and his expression changed. Automatically she started to turn to see what he was looking at. To her horror, a bulky shape was emerging from the dark shadows at the end of the big, empty room. Before she could do more than register that they weren't alone, Erik gave her a hard shove out of the way.

It was all he had time to do. She was fighting to regain her balance when a figure, dressed in raggedy army jacket and fatigues, leaped for Erik. Before Rita's terrified eyes, the two grappled and then crashed to the floor.

"Run!" Erik shouted to her.

Rita had no intention of running away and leaving Erik to fight this...this person. Frantically, she looked around for a weapon of any kind, but the loft was empty of everything but dust. All she had was her big purse. Her friends teased her about carrying everything with her but the kitchen sink, and this was one time she could have used even that. Swinging the heavy purse off her shoulder, she ran over to Erik and his attacker.

The two men were rolling around on the floor, each trying to get a good grip on the other. At least that's what she thought they were doing. It was difficult to tell amid all the grunting and cursing and the wildly swinging arms and the flailing legs. Trying to see through the clouds of dust they were raising, she danced around the struggling duo, swinging the purse by the strap, waiting for the best opportunity to bean the mugger—if that's what he was.

Finally, she saw her chance. The guy in the army jacket managed to get on top of Erik for a second or two, and at the best possible instant, she swung the purse as hard as she could. Her attack caught the man off balance, and he grunted in surprise.

"Take that!" she cried as he crashed to the floor from the force of the blow. She'd hit him right across the back, and for good measure, she swung around and did it again. "And that!"

The second blow did it. Gasping for breath, the man scrabbled away on his hands and knees, then leaped to his feet when he was a safe distance away. As though the hounds of hell were after him, he headed toward the stairs and launched himself down.

Rita didn't wait until the sounds of his clattering departure faded and the front door slammed; Erik was still on the floor, and she threw herself down beside him.

"Are you all right?" she asked anxiously. She saw blood dripping from his cut lip and gasped, "You're hurt!"

"It's nothing," he said. Still trying to catch his breath, he took out his handkerchief and began to swipe at his mouth.

"Give me that!" she commanded when she saw how rough he was being. "You're just going to make it worse."

Taking the handkerchief from him, she gently dabbed away the blood. It was too dim to see much, but she'd been raised with two brothers, and she knew from experience that the injury was just a surface cut.

Thank God! she thought. Now that the episode was over, she felt faint. There was no place to sit except on the gritty floor, but she didn't even think about her suit. Her heart pounding, she plopped down beside Erik, who was sitting there, his legs straight out, balancing on one hand while he gingerly felt his cut lip with the other.

"Wow, that was something, wasn't it?" she said shakily. A thought occurred to her and she gave a quick, frightened look around. "You don't think he has friends up here, do you?"

Erik had apparently already reassured himself that their attacker had been alone. "No, I think he's probably some homeless guy who found a way in and made himself comfortable until we showed up. See that stuff over there? It's probably his."

Rita barely glanced toward the abandoned pile of—whatever it was. Shuddering, she wrapped her arms around her waist. "Poor man."

"Poor man? He tried to attack you."

Rita thought of something else and turned quickly to him. "You saved my life!"

"Hardly," Erik said. He started to grin, then winced when the cut on his lip protested. Touching it briefly again, he shook his head instead. "In fact, I was getting the best of it when you assaulted him."

Remembering how violent and furious that short battle had been, Rita shuddered. "I just caught him off guard. You were the one who—"

"Why didn't you run?"

It had never occurred to her. Indignantly, she said, "I couldn't leave you here alone!"

"You could have been hurt."

"But instead, you were the one." She drew a trembling breath. "That was a brave thing you did, Erik."

"It wasn't brave. I didn't have any choice." He reached for her hand. "I'm just glad you weren't here alone."

The warmth of his fingers was comforting, and she gripped his hand tight. "So am I. I don't know how to thank you, Erik."

"I can think of a way," he said softly.

Gratitude was one thing; what he might be suggesting was quite another. Giving him a sharp look, she said, "Oh?"

He smiled slightly at her tone. "That's not what I meant." They were facing each other on the dirty floor, and still holding on to one of her hands, he reached up and touched her hair.

Without warning, the room seemed even more claustrophobic. A tension sprang to life between them, similar to what she had experienced on the ferry. She knew he wanted to kiss her. What was even more disconcerting was the realization that she wanted to kiss him, too.

It had to be the adrenaline, she thought, trying to convince herself. Even though she had helped to drive off the attacker, she still felt blood rushing through her head, and all her senses were in a heightened state of alert.

Kissing Erik wasn't the way to defuse that tension, she told herself. It would only complicate a situation that was already complicated enough. But despite all her promises to herself, how could she keep her distance from a man who had rushed to defend her?

He'd laughed at her dramatic pronouncement that he had saved her life, but when he had pushed her aside so that he would take the full brunt of the attack, he hadn't known if the man had a weapon or not. In saving her, he could have been seriously hurt, even killed. The thought made her shiver.

"What is it?" he asked anxiously. "You aren't hurt!"

"No, no, I'm okay. It's just . . ."

He got to his feet, pulling her with him. "I think we'd better go."

She clutched his arm. "You don't think he'll come back!"

"And face another attack with a madwoman wielding an assault weapon like that purse?"

"Don't joke!"

When he saw that she was really scared at the thought, he sobered and put an arm around her. "No, I don't think he'll come back. Not right now, anyway. But you never know. I think we should report it, though."

"I hate to do that," she said. She looked around. "Maybe this is the only home he knows."

He shook his head in exasperation. "Women! The guy might have mugged you, or worse, and you're worried about him?"

"I can't help it. He looked so . . . desperate."

Erik grinned lopsidedly. "Then spare some pity for me, because for a while there, I was feeling a little desperate myself."

"You don't need pity," she said, trying to hide her own smile. "What you need is some antibiotic ointment for that cut on your lip."

"Only if you're going to be my nurse. After this experience, I'd rather have you with me than against me."

"Erik," she said suddenly, "you asked if we couldn't just start over."

He didn't even look confused at the abrupt change of subject. "I remember."

"Well..." She hesitated, wondering if she really wanted to do this. Before she could change her mind, she said, "I don't know if starting over is possible, given our...previous relationship. But since we are going to be working together, I'd like to—"

She paused again.

"What?"

It was now or never, she thought, and blurted out, "I'd like to just...go on from here...if you think that's possible."

As though he were afraid her fragile truce offering might shatter, he quickly said, "Do you think that's possible?"

"We can't forget the past—"

"No."

"But it doesn't have to affect our working together."

"I'd like it to be more than that, Rita. I'd like for us to be friends."

Friends? That would have been possible, she thought, if she could forget how she'd felt that night on the ferry.

Still, Erik had put himself in harm's way for her, so she at least owed it to him to try.

"I'd like that," she said.

He paused for a long moment. Then he said, "So would I. Thank you, Rita."

She laughed to break the sudden tension. "I'm the one who should be thanking you. In fact, if I could cook, I'd invite you over for dinner as a way of showing my appreciation."

He laughed, too. "We could go out to dinner again."

She didn't want to touch that one. "It wouldn't be the same," she said hastily. She thought of something that seemed relatively safe. "I know! My parents are about to celebrate their thirty-fifth wedding anniversary at a family picnic. Would you like to go?"

She had issued the invitation half expecting that Erik, the suave sophisticate, would refuse. She would have, in his place. What interest or desire could he have in attending a party with a bunch of strangers whose kids would be running around screaming, most of the time?

But then she recalled another conversation from times gone by. Erik was an only child. In the past, when he had spoken wistfully to her about the joys of belonging to a large family, she had scoffed. As one of seven children, she'd told him he didn't know how lucky he was, but he didn't agree. He'd always wanted brothers and sisters, he'd said, and he'd always wanted to be an uncle to numerous nieces and nephews.

"I'd like that," he told her. "Where and when?"

Oh, she knew what her sisters' reactions were going to be when she brought a man—any man, much less one like Erik—to the party. But in this case, she was just going to have to brave the gauntlet. And why was she worried? she asked herself as she told him the date and time. If anyone asked—and they would, she was sure—all she had to do was tell them that Erik was just a friend.

CHAPTER SIX

THE ANNIVERSARY PARTY for John and Eileen Shannon was held at a park outside San Francisco on a warm and sunny Saturday. The entire family seemed to be there when Rita and Erik arrived, and when Rita saw all the activity, she was glad she had suggested this location. Her two brothers, Terry and Jim, had organized a softball game for the older kids, while her four sisters had put out cloths on the tables and were setting out piles of food from all the baskets and coolers they'd brought.

It was a standing joke in her family that Rita couldn't heat water without burning it, so she had volunteered to bring a huge cake from the bakery. As she and Erik carefully began to remove the big pink box from his car, a horde of younger children saw them and began racing their way with screams of delighted welcome.

"Brace yourself," Rita said with a laugh when she saw the stampede. She glanced at Erik, half expecting to see him recoiling at the wave coming toward them. But he didn't seem the least taken aback; in fact, he was laughing, too, as the kids rushed up.

"Whoa!" he joked as the crowd surrounded them.

It was clear that Rita was a favorite among her numerous nieces and nephews, for they all began to clamor for her attention. There was so much noise and confusion that it was impossible for her to stop and introduce Erik until she held up her hand to silence them.

"Wait!" she cried in mock despair. "You're going to scare off Mr. Mulholland before we even get to the party!"

Her plea barely made a dent in the hubbub.

"Yes, but, Aunt Rita, we want to—"

"Aunt Rita, can you—"

A young girl about ten years old pushed her way forward. She had freckles across the bridge of her nose, and long, blindingly red hair held back from her round face by two barrettes. Her name was Betsy, and she was Marie's oldest. Like most of the children, she was dressed in a T-shirt and shorts. Fixing Erik with huge blue eyes, she asked, "Do you know how to play baseball?"

"I've played a game or two in my time," Erik replied solemnly.

"In that case," Betsy said, "would you teach me how to throw a spitball? I've asked and asked, but the boys won't show me, and I want to learn."

Erik threw an amused glance Rita's way before he hunkered down to the child's level. "I'd be glad to. But why hasn't your Aunt Rita taught you?"

Betsy grinned. "Oh, she knows how to throw a pretty good knuckler, but she just doesn't have what it takes for a real mean spitball."

"I see," Erik said, trying not to laugh. "Well, in that case, maybe we'd better teach her, too."

Rita decided the most dignified approach to this exchange would be to ignore it. Calmly, she said to Erik, "Shall I carry this cake by myself, or are you going to help?"

Erik winked at Betsy and stood up again. He knew that Rita had brought all sorts of things for the kids, as well as several anniversary presents for her parents. All were still in the trunk of his car. Anticipating that she would rather play gift-giver than assign the role to him, he handed her the car keys and took the cake box from her. To the crowd of youngsters, he said, "Your Aunt Rita has some things for you. Why don't you help her out?"

No one needed a second invitation. By the time Rita had passed out new balls and gloves and bats, plus a badminton game and a set of croquet mallets, Erik had joined the adults. As the kids raced away carrying their booty, Rita stopped to watch the scene by the picnic tables.

Even from where she was standing, she could see that Erik was an instant hit. Her four sisters, Marie, Colleen, Martha and Louise, had surrounded him, and even Jim's wife, the shy Stella, had approached. As Rita watched, they all laughed at something he said. Then her brothers and brothers-in-law decided to wander over, and apparently Erik passed muster there, too. By the time Rita joined the other women and her parents, the men had headed back to the baseball diamond and Erik was coaching second base.

"Well!" Marie said slyly when she saw Rita. "Where have you been hiding *him?*"

"I'll second that," Colleen commented with a sideways glance toward the game in progress. Like the other men, Erik was dressed in shirt, jeans and running shoes, but even from this distance, he stood out.

"He's a doll, all right," Martha agreed. She grinned at Rita. "The question is, how did you ever hook him?"

"Now, now, you leave her alone," Louise, the youngest sister said, preparing to defend Rita. Then she laughed. "We all know how hard it is for her to hold on to a man."

"Well, thank you all very much," Rita said pointedly, trying not to laugh, too. "I'll remember your kind comments the next time any of you want me to baby-sit."

Having fired that shot, she went to greet her parents. Giving each of them a kiss, she said, "Happy anniversary, Mom... Dad."

Eileen O'Day Shannon had recently turned sixty. It was from her side of the family that four of her daughters and one of her sons had inherited varying shades of red hair and vivid blue eyes. With their dark eyes and dark hair, Rita and her older brother Terry resembled their father, John. But of the seven children, Rita was the only one who hadn't yet married, and her mother never let her forget it. As Rita straightened from giving her a kiss on the cheek, Eileen's glance went to the baseball field. "I enjoyed meeting your nice young man," she told Rita. "Have you known him long?"

Much too long, and not long enough, Rita thought. But she knew from past experience where this was going, so she replied, "He's just an acquaintance, Mom. Somebody I met through work."

Her sisters came to rescue her. "Speaking of work," Marie said, "how are things going? I've called you several times this past week, but you're never home. I'm beginning to think your new boss is quite the slave-driver."

"She's anything but," Rita told her, with unabashed admiration. "It's just that there's so much to do. You can't believe the details involved in opening up a new store."

"Have you found a location yet?"

"Yes, we have. Just the other day, in fact." Involuntarily, Rita's glance went to Erik again. In today's bright sunshine, their experience with the homeless man seemed distant and long ago. But she could still recall how frightening it had been, and she knew that she would never forget what Erik had done.

Everyone in the family knew by now that Rita was working for Grace DeWilde on a new store, and the women wanted to know all the details.

"Where is the store going to be?" Martha asked. Then she made a face. "Not that I'll be able to shop there, of course. I'm sure it will be totally out of my price range."

"Not to mention the fact that we'll be catering primarily to the bride-to-be," Rita said with a smile. She glanced at Martha's maternity smock and added, "Although after five years of marriage and three and a half kids, maybe Harvey would be glad to marry you all over again."

As though reminded of her state, Martha sat down on the edge of a picnic bench, her hand to her back. She gave a wry grin. "After all this, maybe Harvey would like to start over by himself, period. Now..." she went on, "you were about to tell us more about the store."

Rita was glad to oblige. "It's near Kearny and Post, and Grace just rented the space the other day. But already we've hired a contractor and a store architect. One of the first things they're going to do is sandblast the stone facade. Grace hasn't decided yet about whether or not to leave the wonderful old leaded windows, but one thing is for certain—we're going to gut the inside and rebuild from the ground up."

"That sounds awfully expensive," Marie said.

Once again, Rita glanced over at Erik. This time he was helping one of her nephews with his swing. Rita watched him a moment, touched by the way he was patiently showing the child how to stand and grip the bat. What a wonderful father he would make, she thought. Quickly, she turned away. Now, where had that come from?

"Yes, just getting the building ready is going to cost quite a sum," she said, forcing her thoughts to a safer subject. "But that's what Erik is for. He's getting the financing together."

"From what you've told us about Grace DeWilde," Colleen observed, "you'd think she'd have the financial resources to start something like this by herself."

Rita couldn't discuss Grace's financial situation, even with her family. "It's not done that way. Besides, this store will be separate from all the other DeWildes. In fact, to avoid potential problems and conflicts, it's going to be called Grace."

"Oh, I like that," Marie said. "But wouldn't it be easier—not to mention, guarantee success—if Grace traded on the DeWilde name?"

Again, Rita didn't want to go into her employer's private business. The past week or so had been especially busy with transatlantic phone calls back and forth between Grace and her estranged husband, Jeffrey DeWilde. Grace hadn't said much to her—and of course Rita hadn't directly asked—but she had emerged from several of these telephone conversations agitated and annoyed. It was obvious that Jeffrey, or at least someone in the DeWilde Corporation, was not pleased that Grace had begun the process of opening up her own store.

Because Grace seemed so upset, Rita had dared to ask, "But they can't stop you, can they?"

"No, they can't do that," Grace had replied. "At least, I don't think they can. That's something that Erik and Rudy are going to have to deal with. But I do believe the corporation can make it very difficult for me to use any reference to the DeWilde name in my new business."

"But that's your name, too," Rita had said.

"Only by marriage," Grace had answered wearily. "And since Jeffrey and I haven't started divorce proceedings yet, things are getting complicated. In fact, I'm wondering at this point if I want to have anything to do with brides."

Rita's face fell. Grace saw her expression and quickly said, "I didn't mean that. I'm just a little discouraged right now. I'll get over it." And she had.

"So," Marie asked eagerly, "is Grace's store going to be just a bridal store, or are you going to feature other things?"

"So far, most of our planning revolves around the bride's big day," Rita said. "We'll have the gowns and the veils, the headpieces and the accessories. But we're also talking about having a section of the store devoted to the bride's trousseau. Not the old-fashioned concept that implies, with linens and towels and such—although Grace intends to expand eventually into those, too. We're thinking more in terms of going-away outfits. We would start small, but the store space is big enough that we could enlarge it into themes, like cruise wardrobes, or clothes for ski honeymoons."

Colleen looked delighted. "You mean everything for the wedding and honeymoon, start to finish."

Rita grinned. "Something like that. Everything but the groom!"

"It sounds wonderful," Martha said. "But won't that be awfully expensive, having all those different clothes and things on hand?"

"I did some research on it," Rita said. "I called travel agents and vacation booking services and learned that the most popular honeymoons seem to be cruises or island vacations. Both of which—happily—require similar wardrobes. Or lack thereof," she added wickedly. She beamed at her sisters and her mother. "Grace is wonderful. I wish you could all meet her."

Someone was about to make a comment when a loud cheer erupted at the ball diamond, and they all turned to look. When the women saw that Marie's Betsy had just hit a long ball good enough for a home run, they all cheered, too.

Betsy was so delighted with herself that she rushed over to them after she ran the bases. Hot and sweaty, her cloud of fiery-red hair billowing around her equally red face, the little girl was fiercely victorious.

"I did it!" she cried. "I hit a home run and won the game!"

Marie stood. "That's wonderful, dear. But what happened to your barrettes?"

"Oh, Marie, who cares?" Rita cried, impatient with her sister for once. Grabbing Betsy's hands, she swung her around. "I knew you could do it! Haven't I always told you that girls could play just as well as boys?"

Now that the game had finished, it was time for the kids to eat. Rita helped her sisters settle the youngsters at their own picnic table, so she didn't have time to worry about Erik. She did glance up once to make sure he wasn't alone, and saw that he was deep in conversation with her father and Marie's husband, Hal. Briefly, she wondered what they were talking about, but then she was distracted by the demands of Colleen's twins, Darcy and Dale, who were arguing with one of their cousins about where they were going to sit.

"Now, now," she said. "There's plenty of room for everyone. Why don't you two sit here, and, Tommy, you sit there."

Predictably, all three began to protest. "All right," Rita suggested, "since you don't want to sit down, maybe you'd like to help us serve?"

As they practically raced for their assigned positions, she smiled. She didn't realize that Erik was standing behind her until she turned and almost bumped into him.

"I didn't know you were so good with kids," he said.

"Thanks. But you have to remember how much practice I've had. First with my own brothers and sisters, now with their kids."

"I guess you'll be ready when you have some of your own."

Only half joking, she said, "I'm never having children."

"You don't mean that."

"Yes, I do." She gestured toward the table where her nieces and nephews were jostling one another, stealing food from their cousin's plates, spilling lemonade and generally raising a ruckus. "I've had enough of that to last a lifetime."

"But these kids love you."

"And I love them. But what I like best is that I can always take them home at the end of an outing and give them back to their parents. I couldn't do that with my own." She looked up at him. "Besides, what's with you? You're good with children, too, yet you don't have any."

"Not yet."

Not yet? She wasn't going to consider the implications of that. "Yes, well, it's different for you. You're a man."

"And that means?"

"It means—" She looked around again until she spied the men in the family. Her father and her brothers and her sisters' husbands had all congregated around the barbecue grill, as far away as they could get from the "women and children" without having to move to a completely different park. It was a typical sight at gatherings like this, and she gestured as Marie, Louise and Colleen approached the male group carrying plates laden with food.

"You see that?" she demanded. Erik turned to look, too. When he seemed puzzled—or pretended to be—she explained pointedly, "It's always the same when we have these family occasions. The men *come*—I guess because they know what would happen if they didn't— but they don't do anything but stand around and talk."

"Hold on, that's not true," Erik said, instantly defending his male brethren. "Your brothers organized that ball game, didn't they?"

Rita rolled her eyes. "Big deal. That was *fun*. But where were they this morning when my sisters were in the kitchen cooking up all the food for the picnic? And you notice that they sure aren't volunteering to help serve it—especially to the kids. Why, they can't even walk the few steps to the table to get their own plates. Their wives have to bring the food to them."

"But that's—"

Her eyes narrowed. "If you say that's 'women's work', I'll deck you right here."

He grinned. "After what I saw the other day, I've no doubt you could do exactly that. Actually, I was going to say that not all men are like that."

"Oh, really? The ones I've known are."

"Then you haven't met the right men."

"Are they on this planet?"

He laughed. "Have you ever considered the possibility that maybe men just don't want to get in the way?"

"Oh, pulleeze. If that's their story, I'm sure I speak for the entire female population of the world when I say that we would *all* be more than willing to step immediately to one side and let you guys go to it."

"So you say," he said, trying not to laugh. "But it's my experience that despite all your complaints, you women don't really *want* men to interfere with things you consider your business."

"And where did you learn that particular myth?"

"It's not a myth. It's true. Let me give you an example."

"Oh, please do."

"Okay, let's say that us guys were responsible for planning the picnic today. We were to choose the food, the drinks, everything."

"Go on," she said, crossing her arms.

"Well, since the whole point of getting together is to have fun…" He stopped and grinned at her. "The point *is* to have fun at these things, isn't it?"

She looked at him suspiciously. "I'll concede that. For now."

"Okay, since slaving away in the kitchen isn't *fun,* but since we all still like to eat at picnics, one of us men would have stopped by a fast food place on the way over here and picked up a bunch of hamburgers and french fries and sodas. Someone else would have grabbed some Twinkies and stuff like that from the store. Someone else would have stopped for paper plates—oh, and paper towels, since napkins blow away. When we got here, we'd dump all the food on the table, and in between games, everyone could eat what they wanted, when they wanted. Afterward, we'd scoop up all the garbage into a giant trash bag and throw it in a Dumpster. *That's* how men would give a party.''

Rita had been silent during this recital. When Erik finally came to a halt, she burst into laughter. ''That's the most ridiculous thing I've ever heard!''

''Why? It sounded good to me.''

''That's exactly why men aren't in charge of parties.''

He grinned wickedly. ''I think you just proved my point.''

She was about to give a hot rejoinder when one of her brothers shouted for Erik to join them. ''Gotta go,'' he said. ''My fellow useless males are calling me.''

''Go ahead,'' she replied haughtily. But as he started off, she called after him, ''And don't think you're so smart, Erik Mulholland. Because you just proved *my* point!''

Not the least bit disconcerted, he just waved. She was still standing there staring after him and wondering where the logic in the argument had gone wrong, when Marie joined her.

''Well, you two looked preoccupied just now,'' her sister whispered in her ear. ''Dare I ask what you were talking about?''

Rita looked at her grumpily. "We were talking about the differences between men and women."

Marie looked dismayed. "Oh, Reetz, you didn't get on your soapbox, did you?"

"No, I did not," Rita declared. "I merely pointed out that women always do more work at these gatherings than men do. In fact—"

"I've already heard about the 'in fact,'" her sister said hastily. "Oh, Reetz, *why* do you always do this?"

Rita put her hands on her hips. "What?"

"Don't act so innocent. You know exactly what I mean. Are you deliberately trying to drive him off, too?"

"Like I have all the others, you mean?"

"Don't get mad now."

"I'm not mad! I just don't know why you and everyone else insist on trying to pair me off with some man!"

Marie glanced toward Erik. "I wouldn't say he's just 'some man.'"

"No? It's obvious that he's worked his false charm on the entire family."

"It's not false. He was very sincere when I talked to him."

"You don't know him like I do, Marie. Convincing people that he's *sincere* is what he does for a living. I'd watch out if I were you."

"I don't care what you say. Colleen and Martha and Louise feel the same way. So does Jim's Stella—and Mom, too."

"I might have known you'd all fall for that act of his. You really should get out more, Marie."

Marie looked hurt, and Rita was instantly sorry. "I didn't mean that," she said. "But darn it, Marie, you know I hate it when you start on me about men. I've tried to tell you that Erik is just a business acquaintance. Why don't you believe me?''

"Because I see the way you look at him when he's not looking at you, that's why.''

"What? That's ridiculous!''

"And,'' Marie went on blithely, "I've seen the way he looks at you when you aren't looking. So what do you think of that?''

Rita didn't know what to make of it. Just for a second, she wondered if she was missing something. Instantly, she dismissed the treacherous notion. Marie was a romantic. Given the opportunity, her sister would see love in bloom everywhere. She and Erik were just friends; they had agreed. And she didn't want it to be any more than that. She was perfectly happy the way things were.

But she was quiet in Erik's car on the way home after the picnic finally broke up. So quiet, in fact, that Erik finally looked over at her and asked, "Are you tired or still annoyed with me about what I said earlier?''

She'd forgotten all about that. But since she didn't want to tell him what she was really thinking about, she said, "You have every right to your opinion—just as I do to mine.''

"You are annoyed.''

"No, I'm not.'' She didn't want to talk anymore; she felt too...agitated. What had Marie meant, anyway, when she'd said that Erik *looked* at her in a certain way when she wasn't aware of it? What had Marie seen? Or thought she'd seen?

"You know," Erik said conversationally, "I had a good time today. It was nice to meet your family. And those kids are great."

"That's because they weren't confined," she said contrarily. "You should see them when they're swarming around like a bunch of wild... I don't know what."

He laughed. "From the way you talk, one would think you really *didn't* like kids."

"I've got nothing against kids. I told you. I just don't want any of my own—not now, anyway. I've got too many things I want to do first."

"And children would cramp your style?"

She looked at him indignantly. "It's not a matter of *style*. But don't forget, I know how much time and energy kids take. When—if—I ever have any children, I want to be at the point where they'd come first." She paused. "Men don't have to think like that."

Erik was silent a moment. "I hadn't thought about it in those terms, but you're right. No matter how much a man might *want* to do, no matter how good his intentions, it's still the mother who ends up doing the greater share of the parenting—at least at first. I can understand why you want to plan for a commitment like that."

"You can?"

"Don't sound so surprised. I'm not quite the Neanderthal you picture me. I've learned a few things along the way," he added quietly.

Before she could ask what he meant, they'd turned onto her street. She hadn't intended to ask him in, but the invitation was out before she knew it.

"Would you like to come in for coffee or something?"

"I'd like to, but I've still got a lot of work to do at home, so I'd better get going. But I'll take a rain check, if you're offering."

Rita didn't know whether to be relieved or not that he had refused the invitation. *Damn Marie,* she thought. If her sister hadn't said something about the way she and Erik *looked* at each other, she wouldn't have given today a second thought.

"Anytime," she said, gathering her stuff. He reached for the door at the same time she did. "No, don't bother to get out," she told him. "I can manage."

She started to open the door on her side, but he put a hand on her arm. "I really did have a good time today," he said. "Thanks for asking me."

The light in his eyes made her heart jump. He looked so handsome sitting there behind the wheel, his hair windblown, his face burnished by the sun, and she felt herself being drawn to him whether she wanted to or not. All she had to do, she thought, was lean toward him and . . .

Quickly, she opened the door and got out. From a relatively safe position on the driveway, she was able to bend down and say, "I'm glad you came today, Erik. It was fun."

If he regretted that she had deliberately destroyed— or at least evaded—what could have been a moment, he didn't show it. Instead, he said easily, "Maybe we can do it again sometime."

"I'd like that," she replied, wondering why she was having such trouble holding his gaze. Was it because she was trying to find that "look" Marie had talked about? She blinked and told herself not to be ridiculous. But she had to add, "I'd like that very much."

His eyes darkened, and just for an instant she thought she *had* glimpsed something there. She was certain of it when he said softly, ''So would I.''

She straightened then, before she blurted out something she might regret. But as she watched him drive away, she put her hand to her lips. She should have kissed him, she thought. If she had, she would have gotten over this...this dreadful anticipation. She'd been wondering all afternoon if the old feelings for him were really there, or if she'd just been imagining things. She had finally decided that all she had to do was kiss him to know for sure. But now, when the time had come, she couldn't do it.

Maybe she didn't want to know, she thought as she started into the house. And maybe it was best. She should just leave things as they were: she and Erik were friends, no more, no less.

Wasn't that what she wanted?

She unlocked the front door.

Maybe not.

CHAPTER SEVEN

ON MONDAY MORNING, Erik arrived at his office before 7:00 a.m. He fully intended to dig into the mountain of work on his desk, but when he heard Eleanor bustling around in the reception area and saw that it was nine o'clock, he looked down and realized that he hadn't done a thing. Shoving the papers aside, he stood and went to the window.

He never should have gone to the anniversary party for Rita's parents. He had convinced himself that it was just a family get-together and not a date, but what did it matter? He couldn't stop thinking about Rita.

He'd never seen her like that, not even when they'd known each other before. Last year during their hot, intense and all-too-brief affair, they hadn't had time for anything but each other. But in the company of her brothers and sisters and parents and nieces and nephews, he'd seen a completely different side of her.

And different was hardly the word, he thought. She'd been a surprise from the moment he'd picked her up at her house in Sausalito. The city apartment she'd had last year had been starkly modern; her new place looked like a picture postcard, complete with white picket fence. It hadn't seemed like Rita at all, but after what he'd seen in her Saturday, maybe it was more like her than he realized.

She hadn't even resembled herself that day. He was used to seeing her in suits with high heels, but on Saturday she'd come to the door in bright floral leggings and a white T-shirt, cinched at the hips by a wide leather belt.

He'd still been adjusting to that sight when he realized she'd even changed her hair. Instead of her usual, almost severe wedge, she'd curled it around her face in a style that made her look like a pixie. To say the least, he'd been taken aback by the transformation. She'd looked like a million bucks.

Of course, he hadn't told her so. As they had agreed, he'd kept it simple. Rita had insisted she just wanted to be friends, and he felt that way, too.

This morning, he asked himself how he really felt about Rita Shannon. Then he wondered why it mattered. Their previous relationship was exactly that: *previous*. They'd both moved on. He'd started dating; he presumed she had, too. In fact, he'd found a woman he thought he wanted to marry. So what was the problem?

There *was* no problem. He was simply being influenced by what a good time he'd had with that big family. They were all so close; it was what he wanted—what he'd always lacked—in his own life.

The question was: Could Caroline give him that? He tried to picture it. Caroline had many fine qualities, but donning a T-shirt and leggings and going to a big, old-fashioned picnic in a public park wasn't one of them. Nor could he imagine her doing as Rita had done after lunch: organizing a rousing game of kickball, boys against girls. When her side had won, she had been buried under a pile of delighted little nieces before casually brushing off the grass from her clothes and rejoining the adults. Even with a smudge of dirt on her cheek, she had never looked lovelier to him.

But why was he comparing Caroline and Rita? They were two completely different women. Rita was accustomed to the give-and-take of a big family; Caroline had been raised in quiet decorum. Instead of picnics in the park, she'd attended country club brunches and afternoon high teas.

He couldn't even picture Caroline as a child at that huge place on Russian Hill. The elegant rooms with their precious and valuable furniture were not designed for sticky fingers; the well-bred silences weren't meant to be shattered by the screams of children, no matter how innocent their play.

Two different women, two separate worlds, he thought. That's the way it should be. That's the way it was going to stay.

He was turning back to his desk when his partner knocked on the door and poked his head around.

"Got a minute?" Rudy asked.

"Sure. Come on in."

Rudy was the same age as he was, but with his thinning hair and the thirty pounds he'd gained since college, he looked much older as he came in and sat down. Erik took his chair behind the desk and asked, "What's up?"

"I've been looking into the situation with Grace DeWilde," Rudy said. "And I think we've got some more stormy weather ahead."

"I'm not sure I like the sound of that. What's happened?"

"I was hoping the DeWilde Corporation would be content just to make some noise about Grace's plans,"

Rudy told him, "but I just got a fax that hints they might be more seriously inclined to stop her."

"In what way?"

"They're considering a suit against her."

"On what basis? They can't prevent her from opening her own store."

"No, but they can tie us up in court. She's already decided not to use the name, but there is the exclusivity angle—not to mention the competition problem and the non-compete clauses. We can fight all those, of course, and probably win. But it will be a headache."

"How much of a headache? How long are we talking about?"

"Who knows these days? Weeks? Months? Years? It depends on how far they want to take it. It could be that the husband is just being vindictive. Or it could be that the corporation recognizes that she could be a threat and will decide to protect its interests. They have a battery of lawyers to make it difficult."

"Fine. We can make things difficult, too."

"That's true," Rudy agreed. "But unless I miss my guess, Grace doesn't have the resources to fight them if they want to go to the mat."

Erik thought a moment. "She's got that block of stock."

"But she doesn't want to sell it yet." Rudy pondered a moment. "However, *they* don't have to know that. We could use it as a lever."

"Or a threat," Erik agreed. He sat back. "So, what do you suggest? Wait until they make a move, or anticipate them and make one ourselves?"

"I have a few ideas I want to try. But I'm going to advise her to be prepared. If they do decide to fight her, they can erect so many road blocks that even when we do clear them away, the money might be scared off. And then where will she be?"

"Leave the finance end of it to me. You worry about the legalities."

Rudy nodded and got to his feet. He started toward the door, but on the way he stopped and looked back at Erik. "On a lighter note, how was the weekend?"

Erik knew he shouldn't have told his partner that he was going to the anniversary party with Rita. Rudy knew all about their affair last year—how badly it had ended, and how responsible Erik had felt.

"It was fine," he said noncommittally.

"Fine? That's all?"

"Well, it wasn't a date."

"Oh, I get it. It was more of a family-oriented business meeting in a park. Sort of like a company picnic, but without the company."

"Are you trying to be cute?"

"Are you trying to be evasive?"

"I'm not being evasive. I told you the truth. It was okay—if you like barbecued ribs and yelling kids."

"Not me." Rudy shuddered. He was twice-divorced with no children, and now he intended to stay a bachelor the rest of his life.

"So you see? All we did was play baseball and—"

"Spare me the child-oriented details. I want to know how things are with Rita. After all, last year you didn't really part on the best of—"

"That's past history. I'm involved with Caroline now."

Rudy sighed. "I was trying to forget about that."

"Oh?"

Rudy saw his expression and held up a hand. "Forget it. I shouldn't have said anything."

"But you did, so you might as well go on with it. What did you mean?"

Rudy hesitated before he said, "We've been friends for a long time—"

"And now you're going to say something that's going to jeopardize that long-standing friendship."

"I hope not. It's... Well, look—I just don't know what you see in Caroline Madison. Forgive me, but she doesn't seem to be your type."

"What are you saying? She's exactly my type!"

"Come on, Erik. She's... boring."

Erik stiffened. "Since when are you an authority?"

"Perhaps you're right. I did have two wives—neither of whom dotes on me like Caroline does on you."

"And that's bad?"

"No, it's good—if you're the King of Siam. But I can't believe you're really interested in a woman who clings to your every word and gesture. Don't you want more of a challenge?"

"Now you're psychoanalyzing me?"

"I don't need to be a therapist to see that Caroline just isn't the woman for you. You've just been sort of...rolling along ever since you met her. Then you start seeing Rita again, and—"

"I'm not seeing Rita!"

"Whatever you want to call it, the fact remains that you haven't been this...*alive* in a long time." Rudy paused. "Since the last time you were seeing Rita, in fact."

"You don't know what you're talking about."

"Don't I? Ask yourself this, then. If Caroline is really the one for you, why do you keep putting off the big question? You've had that ring for weeks now. Have you asked her to marry you yet?"

Try as he might, Erik couldn't hold his partner's eyes. "I just haven't found the right time, that's all."

"Bull. You haven't asked her because you know in your heart that she's not the woman for you. Now, you and Rita—"

"Will you get off the subject of Rita Shannon? I told you, Rudy. That relationship is in the past—where it's going to stay!"

Rudy wouldn't drop the subject. "I'm not so sure about that. In fact, do you know what I think?"

"No, and I don't want to know."

As though he hadn't spoken, Rudy went on. "I believe you were already in love with Rita when that Glencannon thing got out of hand. Sometimes I think—"

"I already know what you think about that, so let's not discuss it again, shall we? And you're wrong, Rudy. Dead wrong."

"I don't think so," Rudy persisted. "I always did believe that things would have turned out differently if you'd told Rita what really happened."

Erik looked up sharply. There were only three people in the world who knew the true story about the Glencannon-Maxwell takeover, and he and Rudy were two of them.

"I told you," Erik said with finality. "I don't want to talk about it."

Rudy wasn't intimidated. Shrugging again, he said, "Fine, don't. But until you do talk about it, it's always going to be there in the background, spoiling any chance you and Rita might have to get back together."

"Rita and I are *not* going to get back together. I've told you, Caroline is the woman for me."

His partner threw up his hands. "All right, all right, I give up. But I still think you're making a mistake."

"Fine," Erik said heavily. "It's my mistake to make."

Sighing, Rudy headed toward the door. But before he opened it, he paused again. "I almost forgot. Have you heard the scuttlebutt about Phil Soames?"

Erik tensed at the mention of that name. He and Phil Soames went back a long way. Once, they had been the best of friends, but that was in the past, too. When Erik pictured blond, blue-eyed, lady-killer Phil, the man who charmed his victims even as he was taking them to the cleaners, his jaw tightened even more. Phil now owned Los Angeles-based Soames and Associates, an investment firm like Mulholland-Laughton. But last year Phil had been in San Francisco, during the time of the Glencannon takeover.

"What about him?" he asked stiffly.

"Rumor has it that Phil is maneuvering to put together the financing for that international Sutcliff construction project," Rudy said.

Erik sneered. "His company hasn't been around long enough to get a project like that."

"I don't know. I heard the other day that he's one of the front-runners."

"In his dreams, maybe. He always was a legend in his own mind."

"I don't blame you for curling your lip like that. But it's possible he might do it."

"Never in a million years. That project has to be solid to get off the ground, and Phil has a reputation for cutting too many corners."

"Maybe he's learned his lesson."

"Yeah, and I can fly to Monaco under my own power."

Rudy's gaze was keen. "He's pulled things off before."

Erik had to force himself to meet his partner's eyes. "No one knows that better than I do. But that was then. Sutcliff is different."

"Whatever you say. I hope you're right."

"I know I am."

But Erik wasn't so certain after Rudy returned to his own office. He'd heard about the Sutcliff project—who in his field hadn't? The plan was to build a worldwide chain of hotels linked by theme, utilizing both workers and materials indigenous to the areas where the hotels were to be constructed. The idea was to promote tourism, but also to give local people a chance to work—before, during and after construction. It was a vast undertaking, requiring almost unlimited capital and equally limitless vision. The financing alone would be a nightmare, commanding the complete attention of anyone fortunate enough to land the account.

He'd been interested when he'd first heard about it, but he and Rudy agreed they already had too many balls in the air, so he hadn't actively pursued it. Now that he knew Phil was on the hustle, he wondered if they should look into it again.

That was ridiculous. Was his resentment of Phil Soames—no, his hatred, he thought; he might as well admit it—going to make him turn the office upside down for a dubious pursuit? Mulholland-Laughton had more work than they could handle now; just because Phil might become involved in the Sutcliff project didn't mean that *he* had to get on his horse and start riding off in all directions.

"Forget it," he muttered. He wasn't going to start brooding on the wrongs Phil had done to him or he'd never get any work done. He reached for the phone. Eleanor had brought in a stack of old-fashioned messages for him, and he had to answer a backlog of voice mail. He might as well get to it.

The first message was an urgent request from a man named Chuck Yakimoto, one of the group of Asian businessmen who had visited him last week. He glanced at the number Chuck had given and began to dial, only to change his mind halfway through. He broke the connection and dialed another number instead.

"Grace DeWilde's office. How may I help you?"

"Hi, Rita," he said. "This is Erik."

"Hi," she answered, her voice warming. "Oh, I'm sorry, but Grace isn't here."

"That's okay. I called to talk to you. I wanted to thank you again for inviting me to your parents' anniversary party. I had a great time."

"I'm glad. But in all the rush, I forgot to say that you really didn't have to give them that beautiful statuette. When I invited you, I didn't intend for you to bring a gift."

"It's not every day that two people celebrate thirty-five years together. It was an occasion to commemorate. And it wasn't so much."

"Yes, it was. My mother loved it, and even my father, who rarely says anything, was impressed. It was so thoughtful of you."

"I'm glad they liked it."

He was about to say something more, but just then an image came to his mind. The party had lasted until very late in the afternoon; by the time they'd all headed home, it was early evening, when the world around them was touched by a golden light. Rita had been sitting beside him in the car, her eyes closed, her head against the seat. In that radiant sunset, her skin had seemed to glow, and he'd wanted to kiss her so badly he ached.

Just thinking about it made him feel hot all over again, and he loosened his tie. Then, without any warning at all, he found himself saying, "I'd like to reciprocate, if I may. *The Phantom of the Opera* is at the Curran, and one of my clients has a box he can't use this weekend. Would you like to go?"

"Oh, Erik, I—"

He knew she was trying to think of a graceful way to refuse, and he couldn't blame her. The family picnic was one thing; an invitation to the theater could only be construed as a date—something friends didn't do. He wished he'd thought of that before he'd blurted out the offer. Even though Caroline didn't want to go, and had told him so, he should have let the box go to waste. Quickly, he said, "Forget it. I bet you've probably seen the show a dozen times."

Her voice sounded strange. "Actually, I've never seen it." She hesitated. "I'd love to go. There's just one problem—"

"You don't have to explain," he said, backpedaling as fast as he could. "It was only a thought. I should have realized you had other plans."

"No, it's not that. It's just that this weekend I agreed to take care of Betsy."

"The red-headed fireball who's headed for the major leagues?"

Rita laughed. "Yes, the one you taught to throw that blistering spitball. Anyway, even though I'm sure that—

at the grand old age of ten years—she would vehemently disagree, I couldn't leave her home by herself."

"Do you think she would enjoy the show?"

"Enjoy it? She's such a ham she'd probably want to be onstage singing the lead."

"Well, then, bring her along. We'll have a box, so there will be plenty of room."

"Oh..." Again, that hesitation. "That's very generous of you, Erik. But when I said that, I didn't mean to invite her."

"*I* invited her. And it will be fun."

"Fun?" she repeated weakly. "I don't think you realize what you're getting into. Betsy can be quite a handful."

"It seems to run in the family," he said. Then, lest she misconstrue, he added, "Anyway, I'm not worried. I'll see you ladies this weekend."

He hung up the phone and didn't realize he was grinning until Eleanor came into the office and said, "You look pleased. I take it that phone call was a success?"

"I guess you could say so. As it stands now, I'm going to be escorting two women to the theater on Saturday night."

"Two? Well, I hope you have a good time with Caroline and her mother."

Erik knew he should correct her mistaken impression, but he didn't. The day wore on, and he concentrated on his work. But as he packed up to go home, he suddenly realized that he wasn't thinking of Caroline Madison or even Phil Soames, the man he would have given anything to ruin.

Instead, he was remembering the Shannon picnic again. After he had shown Betsy how to throw a ball that the boys would have trouble hitting, he had helped

another child named Todd with his batting swing. He
had enjoyed that, and he wondered again what it would
be like to have children of his own.

He'd like a son, of course. What man wouldn't? But
even more, he wanted a little girl—one with a saucy grin
that would be his downfall. He could see her now: she'd
have dark hair and dark eyes and would look just like
her mother.

It wasn't until he was in the car and on his way home
that he realized his mistake. Caroline had blond hair
and blue eyes. And yet the daughter he had pictured as
his looked just like Rita Shannon.

CHAPTER EIGHT

"FORGIVE ME, GRACE," Howard Hunnicut said, "but you seem a little nervous. Have I done something to make you uncomfortable?"

"Of course not," Grace said quickly. She hadn't realized that she had allowed her preoccupation to show, and she placed an apologetic hand on her old friend's arm. "Forgive me, please. It's not you. It's wonderful to see you again after all these years. I guess I just have too much on my mind these days."

They were having lunch at Mallory's, her niece's restaurant near Union Square. It was now midsummer, and the city was sweltering in a miniheat wave. But the restaurant had the air-conditioning going full blast, and Grace shivered slightly, pulling her short-sleeved jacket a little closer.

"It's good to see you, too, Grace," he said, returning her smile. "You look wonderful, in spite of—" He stopped, his face reddening. "I'm sorry. I shouldn't have mentioned it."

"Don't be silly." Grace knew that he'd been about to say something about her and Jeffrey, and she sighed. "I'd rather people come right out and say something. It would make things so much less awkward. And after all, my separation from Jeffrey is no secret. Heaven knows, the media had a field day with it."

"I can only imagine how difficult it's been," Howard said. "I remember how hard it was when Dora and I divorced, and we didn't have to do it in the full glare of the public eye."

"It's amazing what stuff tabloids will print even when there's not a shred of truth to it." She grimaced. "And the mainstream press here is almost as bad. In fact, I'm surprised you had the courage to call and ask me to lunch. The way I've been portrayed lately in some of the more lurid tales, I'm a modern-day witch."

Howard laughed. He was a man of medium height with brown hair and kind blue eyes. Grace had known him since high school, and when he had called to ask if she remembered him, and to suggest they have lunch, she had immediately accepted. Even though there was nothing remotely physical between them, it felt good to be going out with an accommodating man again, and she had basked in the attention until she remembered that Kate was coming to talk to her. It seemed that her youngest daughter had been delegated to discuss the "situation" and report back to her two siblings.

"It's been rough, I know," Howard said. He placed his hand carefully over hers. "Is there anything I can do for you?"

Grace was again grateful for the gesture—and the offer. But she said, "Thank you, no. I wish there was, though. Things seem so much more complicated now than when I came. But still, I have this project of mine. It takes up much more time than even I anticipated."

She'd told him about her new store, and he asked, "How are things going?"

Glad to change the subject to something a little less personal, she said, "I haven't a clue as to when we'll actually open, but the rebuilding is going well, and soon—thank the Lord!—we'll have actual *office* space. I like my new apartment, and there is room to work there, but I do prefer to keep my business and my private lives separate."

"I agree. It's always best that way."

"Yes, it is," Grace said, then laughed. "And I also have to confess that even though I'm fond of my assistant, she and I are getting quite tired of bumping into each other in the living room."

"You were fortunate to find store space in such a plum location. I'm sure that will make a big difference when you open."

She smiled fondly. "I have Erik Mulholland to thank for that. He's the one who found out about the place before it went on the market."

"Erik Mulholland," Howard repeated, frowning slightly. "I know I've heard that name before."

"Well, I may have mentioned him. And you've probably read about him in the business section of the newspaper. He's involved with that Asian group from Ishitaki. They want to build a hotel."

Howard grimaced. "Just what we need."

"Erik says that, too. But the hotel is just one of his projects. Recently, he's bought and sold several large computer companies in the Silicon Valley."

"I hope he's taking good care of you."

"Oh, he is. I don't know what I would have done without him and his partner, Rudy Laughton. They've both been such a help, especially when Jeffrey and the board became somewhat . . . difficult."

"I take it Jeffrey doesn't want you as a rival?"

"To say the least," Grace said with a shudder. "Though I hardly consider myself a rival when the only DeWilde store in North America is in New York. I wanted to open a San Francisco store even when I was part of the DeWilde Corporation. But somehow we never had the time—or made the time—to look into it. Now I have the opportunity, and nothing Jeffrey or anyone else can say is going to stop me."

Howard smiled. "You haven't changed, Grace. You always were a spitfire."

"I'll take that as a compliment," she said, returning his smile. "But to be fair, I have to give Jeffrey his due. I was fortunate. Even in family-owned and operated companies, women don't always get the chance they deserve. Everyone at DeWilde's was very good to me. I was allowed to do just what I wanted."

He wasn't convinced. "I think you underestimate both your own business acumen and your contribution to the stores."

She made a wry face. "I have to say, it was much easier with the corporation behind me. There are times when I think I'll never get this San Francisco store off the ground. It's been one delay, one problem after the other."

"You'll overcome them all. Soon you'll open to great acclaim and much fanfare."

She laughed. "At this point, I'd settle for not falling flat on my face."

"I doubt you'd ever do that."

She happened to glance at her watch. "Good heavens, look at the time. I'm sorry, Howard, but I have to cut this short."

"So soon? We've barely had a chance to catch up on old times."

"I know. But I really do have to get back. I'll tell you what. Why don't we go to dinner . . . soon?"

Reluctantly, he signaled for the check. "I'll hold you to that."

They went outside, where he flagged down a cab. As he held the door for her, he said, "I'll call you again."

"I hope so, Howard. I enjoyed lunch, really."

"So did I." He touched her hand briefly before the taxi pulled away, and she felt a glow as she directed the driver to the marina, where her apartment was located. She'd needed something to give her a lift, and Howard Hunnicut had been just the person to do it.

The cab dropped her off, and she was still smiling as she unlocked the apartment door. "Rita!" she called. "I'm back from lunch. Oh, it was—"

She stopped. Her youngest daughter had been sitting on one of the couches in the living room. When Grace came in, she stood, hands on her hips, and said, "Well, you're finally here, Mother. Where have you been?"

Grace shut the door. "I've been out to lunch with an old friend named Howard Hunnicut."

She had hardly seen Kate since she came to San Francisco, Grace thought. Kate was completing her medical residency, and it seemed to Grace that she worked night and day. The only time she had off was used for much-needed sleep. Trying not to think how tired and pale her daughter looked, Grace gave her a hug. Then she stepped back and searched her face.

"You look upset, darling," she said carefully. "What's wrong?"

"Mother, we have to talk."

"Of course. But first, I'd like to speak to Rita...." She looked around. "Where is she?"

"She went to lunch."

"And left you here alone?"

"Well, Mother, I hardly think she suspected I'd steal the silver," Kate said impatiently. But when she saw Grace's face, she added, "To be honest, she didn't want to go, but I insisted. However, I never expected that you'd be gone so long. I thought I was going to have to head back before I saw you."

"Well, then, it's fortunate I came back when I did," Grace said. "And now that we're both here, how about some tea? Then we can talk about what you came to tell me, you can report back to your brother and sister, and all will be well."

"You make fun, Mother," Kate said darkly as she followed Grace into the kitchen, "but the truth is that Gabe and Meg and I are all worried about you and Dad."

Grace began to collect the tea things. She didn't want any tea, but the process gave her time to get her thoughts in order and to steady her nerves. She was sure she wasn't going to like this inquisition, however well-intentioned, but she knew she had to listen. It was just that Kate was always so *intense,* she thought with resignation.

"I appreciate that you're concerned," she said as she held the kettle under the tap for water. "But to be honest, this is between your father and me, and there's nothing, really, that any of you can do."

Kate's voice rose. "But we don't understand why—"

Grace turned to her. Forgetting the tea, she took her daughter's hands and said quietly, "I don't understand why, either. But you're just going to have to let your father and I work this out, in our own way and our own time."

Kate's beautiful face twisted. Grace had always felt a fierce pride and love for all her children. She still did, even though at present, Megan was being a little stand-offish, and Gabriel had hurt her deeply both by his elopement and his unwavering estrangement.

But in her heart of hearts, where no one but she was admitted, Grace had to confess to a special affection for her youngest child—this daughter of autumn colors, with her vivid green eyes and auburn hair. When she saw Kate's obvious distress, she drew her over to the table and gently pressed her into a chair.

"Kate, darling," she said, "please don't cry—"

"I'm not crying!" Kate exclaimed, tears filling her eyes. "You know I hate to cry!"

She grabbed a napkin from the table and blotted her eyes. "It's just so unbelievable! We all thought that you and Dad would go on forever. You seemed to have the perfect marriage."

"No one has the perfect marriage, Kate. You should know that."

"I do know. I just said that it *seemed* perfect. But what happened, Mother? One minute, everything was fine, and the next..."

Grace had been debating about how much to tell her children and had finally decided that she could only tell her part of the story. The rest of it had to come from Jeffrey. After all, he was the one who had had the affair; it was his betrayal that had finally driven them apart.

But she wasn't innocent, either, and so she said quietly, "I made a mistake, darling. I told your father..." She lost courage for a moment. Did she really want to get into this? Then she looked at Kate's tragic eyes and knew that if she didn't, her children would never understand or forgive her. She couldn't bear the thought.

"I've never told anyone this before, Kate," she said, "but before I explain . . . or try to . . . you must understand that I was brought up to believe that the most important thing I could do was to marry well."

"Oh, Mother!"

"I know, I know, it's not that way now. Thank goodness things have changed. But back then . . . well, you have to realize how it was. My family was old-line San Francisco, awash with social pretensions but lacking the wherewithal to fund them. It's not that we were poor—as you know, I went to London to study. But our financial situation could have been a bit more secure."

"But what does that have to do with you and Dad?"

Grace started to answer, but just then, her memory flashed back to the night she had first seen Jeffrey, at the London University annual student ball. She'd been barely twenty, and he was five years older. He'd been so handsome, she thought dreamily, so sure of himself—outwardly, at least. And she'd been so delighted when he'd deigned to notice her!

With an effort, she returned to the present. Kate was still looking at her expectantly, so she gathered her thoughts and confessed, "I wasn't sure I loved your father when I married him. Looking back on it, I think I loved the *idea* he represented. After all, he came from a socially prominent family—"

"You married him for money!" Kate was scandalized.

"No, no," Grace said quickly. "It was just that I was so . . . overwhelmed by him. He wasn't the man of my dreams—he was so much more. I was dazzled by him. It took me a while to realize that I really *did* love him, that I was *passionately* in love with him."

"But if you felt that way . . . Mother, do you still love him?"

"I'll always love him. But now things are complicated. As I said, last New Year's Eve, I made the mistake of telling your father what I just told you. Foolishly, I thought that after all these years we'd laugh about how silly I'd been back then, and how young. But your father didn't react the way I'd expected. Instead, he was hurt and angry. The fact that I'd quickly sorted out my feelings for him back then—and had grown to love and respect him more with every year—didn't seem to matter. He felt betrayed. He couldn't forgive me."

"But that's not fair!"

Wearily, Grace pushed back a strand of hair. "No," she agreed, "it's not. But that's the way it is."

Kate was silent a moment. "There's something you're not telling me, isn't there?"

Grace couldn't lie to her. "Yes, there is. But if you want more, you're going to have to ask your father."

"Now you're not being fair!"

"I'm sorry, Katie. But I can't speak for your father and you know it. I never have, and I won't start now."

"This is such a mess!"

Grace couldn't have agreed more. "I know you're upset. We all are. But we'll get through this. It will just take time."

Kate crushed the napkin in her hand. "Are you saying that you don't think you and Dad will ever get back together?"

"I don't know," Grace said quietly. "It's hard to say what will happen."

"Well, if this is the way things are, I'm *never* getting married!"

Wisely, Grace decided to ignore that melodramatic statement. She was trying to think of something comforting to say when Rita appeared on the threshold. Looking as though she'd rather be any place but there, she said, "I'm sorry to interrupt, Grace, but a man named Nick Santos is here. I told him he should make an appointment, but he said your husband sent him. He's insisting on talking to you."

Grace didn't know a Nick Santos. And at the moment, she didn't care to. She was more interested in trying to console her daughter. "Tell him he'll have to wait."

"Will do," Rita said. She glanced at Kate, who had averted her face. "Is everything . . . ?"

"Everything's fine," Grace said reassuringly. "Tell Mr. Santos I'll be out directly."

When Rita left, Grace turned her attention to her daughter once more. "Come on now, Katie. It's not the end of the world. . . ."

"It sure seems like it," Kate said mournfully. She wiped away a tear. "I feel so silly, breaking down like this." She sniffed and straightened. "Someone's here to see you, so go ahead. I'll be all right."

"You're more important, darling. I'd rather stay with you."

"No, it's okay. I'll get myself together and come out in a second."

Grace didn't want to leave her like this. "If you still want to talk—"

"Of course I want to talk. But you've made it clear that I have to speak to Dad first."

"Now, Kate—"

"I didn't mean it like that. I'm sorry. I'm still trying to adjust to all this, I guess."

"I understand. We all are." Grace smoothed back Kate's fiery hair and kissed her forehead.

Kate grabbed her mother's hand and gave it a little squeeze. "You go ahead and find out what this Mr. Sampros wants. I'll be right out."

It wasn't *Sampros*, but Santos, as Grace found out a moment later when she went into the living room to meet him. As she walked in, the man who had been sitting on the couch rose. It took him a while to do so, for he was at least three inches over six feet. As he unfolded himself and stood, Grace saw that he seemed to be in his early thirties. Dark-haired and dark-eyed, he was wearing a light-colored suit, a white shirt and a blue-and-gold tie.

Grace preferred men who were fair, but she had to admit that Nick Santos was a good-looking man. With his swarthy complexion, high cheekbones and fierce, compelling eyes, she couldn't pin down his nationality, but if she had to guess, she'd say he was a winning combination of Spanish or Portuguese, with perhaps a hint of French thrown in to make things even more interesting. He wore his black, wavy hair just long enough to curl over his ears and down to his collar, and as he turned her way, he suddenly reminded her of the part-Latino actor currently starring on television in a New York police show.

"Mrs. DeWilde?" he said before Rita could introduce them. "My name is Nicholas Santos—Nick, if you please. Your husband has hired me to look into a matter of some importance, and I'd like to speak to you privately for a moment, if that's possible."

There was a lilt to his deep voice that wasn't quite an accent. Charmed despite the mention of Jeffrey, Grace said, "I have a few minutes, Mr. Santos." She looked around and realized there wasn't really a private place to talk. "I'm afraid we'll have to have our discussion in here."

"I'll go and make some tea," Rita offered. "And perhaps see if Kate—"

But Kate herself appeared just then. She started to say, "I'm off, Mother. I'll see—"

She stopped when she saw Nick Santos. In one of those unfathomable moments that sometimes happen when two people meet for the first time, his dark eyes held hers for a beat longer than necessary. To Grace's amazement, Kate actually blushed.

"Well..." Kate said, obviously flustered. "I didn't mean to interrupt."

Grace rescued her. "Kate, this is Nick Santos. Mr. Santos, my youngest daughter, Dr. Kate DeWilde."

The two shook hands, murmuring the usual pleasantries, but it was obvious that something was happening. As though she'd forgotten that she had just announced she was leaving, Kate sat down. Nick sat, too. He couldn't seem to take his eyes from her.

Trying to hide a smile—although she didn't know why, since no one was paying any attention to her—Grace took a seat, too. Tactfully, Rita excused herself. When her assistant was gone, Grace said, "Now, Mr. Santos, what can I do for you?"

He had to drag his glance away from Kate. As though suddenly remembering Grace was the reason he had come, he said, "I'm not sure you can do anything. But first, I think I should identify myself, so you'll be certain I am who I say I am."

While they were digesting the implications of those words, he reached into his jacket and pulled out a wallet. He opened it and showed them his identification. In one compartment was his California driver's license; in the other was a different kind of license. When Grace saw what it was, she put a hand to her throat, but Kate immediately pounced.

"You're a private investigator?" She made it sound almost like an accusation. She turned to Grace. "Mother, do you know anything about this?"

Grace hadn't a clue. "No, I—"

Nick put the wallet away. His dark gaze held Kate's for a moment, then he looked at Grace. "I'm sorry to be so blunt, but time is of the essence. Recently, a tiara showed up at an antique dealer's in New York. It appears to be part of the missing DeWilde collection. Do you know anything about it?"

Grace knew all about the story of the missing DeWilde jewels. Every member of the family had been sworn to secrecy, but Jeffrey had told her the tale years ago. According to the scant information pieced together by Charles, Jeffrey's father, someone had reportedly stolen six of the most valuable pieces in the collection. No one was quite sure who, but family members had always suspected one of their own. And Jeffrey's uncle Dick had vanished about the same time....

That was in the late forties, when insider gossip had been even more deadly than the tabloid press was today. DeWilde's was an established institution; if discovered, the scandal would have ruined the reputation of the stores and the family. So the incident had been quickly hushed up and, hopefully, forgotten. To hear that one of the missing pieces had surfaced was a shock, and Grace didn't know what to say.

"I... I can't believe it," she finally said. "The story of those jewels has attained almost mythic status in the family by now. To tell the truth, I almost believed the pieces weren't even real."

Nick smiled tightly. "Oh, they're real, all right. And now, after almost fifty years, this tiara has appeared. Your husband has hired me to find out why."

"I see." Grace got up and went to the window. She stared out across the marina for a moment before she turned back to the investigator. "How can I help you? I don't know anything about the jewels, missing or otherwise. And I certainly hadn't heard about the appearance of the tiara."

"Neither has anyone else—or so it seems, at present. Your husband would like to keep it that way until I'm finished with my investigation. By then, I'll have the whole story."

"How?" Kate challenged. She had never been told the story of the missing jewels, but she wasn't going to admit that in front of Nick Santos. She would grill her mother later. "If those pieces have supposedly gone missing for nearly half a century, how are you going to find the rest of them now?"

"Kate," Grace murmured. She was still trying to adjust to this extraordinary news. "Why don't we allow Mr. Santos to tell us his own way?"

"Thank you, Mrs. DeWilde," Nick said. He looked at Kate with those smoldering eyes again. "To answer your question, the appearance of the tiara is the starting point, of course. I'll work back from that to the source. Someone knows something. It's my job to track that person, or persons, down. I *will* find them. And when I do..."

His tone was vaguely menacing, and Grace had no doubt that he would do exactly as he promised. Before Kate could jump in again, she said quickly, "I'm sure you will solve this mystery. But how can I help? I told you, I don't know anything about it.''

''I'm sure that's true,'' he said. ''But I came to ask—''

Despite her mother's admonition, Kate was roused once more. ''You sound like you don't believe her!''

He turned deferentially to her again. Two flares of color appeared in her cheeks, but Kate stared right back at him. Holding her eyes with a look that was so intense that even Grace was aware of it from across the room, he said to Kate, ''On the contrary, I always believe what people tell me—until I can prove otherwise. And I have no reason to doubt what your mother says.''

''Thank heaven for that,'' Grace said lightly, trying to relieve the tension. As startled as she was by this new development with the jewels, she was amused at the byplay between the big detective and her youngest child. She'd never seen Kate act like this, and she was fascinated.

Nick turned back to her. ''I did have another purpose in visiting you, Mrs. DeWilde. And you, Dr. DeWilde,'' he added for Kate's benefit.

Kate's green eyes narrowed. ''And what purpose was that, Mr. Santos?''

''According to the information I've been given about the DeWildes—''

The green eyes flashed. ''What information are you talking about? Who gave you the right to pry into our family?''

With a smile playing about his sensuous mouth, he said, ''Your father. To do my job properly, I need to know everything I can about your family, so Mr. DeWilde gave me dossiers on everyone. All with the understanding, of course, that the material was to remain strictly confidential.''

''I'm not sure I like that,'' Kate said. She turned to Grace. ''Mother, what do you think of this?''

Grace didn't know what to think. Jeffrey was one of the most obsessively private people she had ever known. For him to have given out any details at all about any member of the family had to mean he was seriously concerned.

And well he should be, she thought. The family had kept the theft of the missing DeWilde jewels a secret all these years. She could imagine the turmoil at corporation headquarters when the tiara had surfaced in New York. How were they going to explain it?

It wasn't any of her business. Even though a myriad of details still had to be worked out, she was no longer involved in the workings of the DeWilde Corporation. The realization made her sad and angry at the same time, and in a surge of resentment, she told herself she didn't care if Jeffrey and Company were all singed in this fire of their own making. If the family hadn't been so fanatically determined to protect one of their own, this wouldn't have happened.

She looked at the detective. ''You said you had another purpose in coming here, Mr. Santos.''

He sensed the change in her; she could see it in the sudden speculation in his eyes. But he merely said, ''I did. Your husband...er, Mr. Jeffrey DeWilde has requested cooperation from everyone in the family. So if you hear or think of anything, please contact me. I'll be traveling around quite a lot, but I can be reached through this number....''

He pulled out a card and put it on the coffee table. Before Grace could get it, Kate leaned forward and snatched it up. "You won't mind if I call my father and confirm this, will you?" she challenged.

He seemed amused at that, too. "Be my guest, Doctor." He turned to Grace. "In the meantime, do you have any questions, Mrs. DeWilde?"

Grace had dozens of questions, none of which she intended to direct to Nicholas Santos. She shook her head. "No, not at the moment."

He nodded and stood. Kate jumped up, too. Although she was five foot six herself, she seemed almost petite next to his great size. It seemed to annoy her further that she had to look up at him, and she demanded, "When you do find those responsible— *if* you do, of course—what will happen to them?"

Nick looked down at his inquisitor. To Grace, watching with such interest, it seemed that he was about to reach for Kate, to touch her face or pull her toward him. He didn't move, but Grace could have sworn that he *leaned* toward her daughter. For a crazy moment, she wondered if he was going to bend down and kiss her.

Kate seemed to feel it, too, for she stepped quickly back. Grace realized then just how affected Kate was by this man and was even more intrigued. She had never seen that particular expression on her daughter's face before.

What is happening here? she wondered. The tension between Kate and Nick seemed to have taken on a life of its own. Without a word being spoken, it was obvious that something was going on.

Then Rita broke the spell between the two by returning innocently to the room. With her appearance, the atmosphere changed again, and things proceeded as they should. The detective said goodbye, and as Rita showed him out, Grace turned to her daughter.

Kate was still watching Nick, her glance running down the length of his long body. A tiny frown appeared between her silky eyebrows when she noted his slight limp.

"Well," Grace said, "that was interesting, don't you think?"

"Interesting?" Kate's already vivid color was still high. When she turned to her mother, her eyes were like jade. Even her hair seemed to crackle. "You mean about the tiara? Yes, I suppose so. I haven't time now, Mother, but one day soon I want to be filled in about this deep, dark secret of the family jewels." She sniffed. "I can't say I think much about that investigator, though. He seems pretty cocky to me." She turned to Rita, who had rejoined them. "What do you think?"

Rita glanced from mother to daughter. It was clear that she didn't want to get into the middle of this. Neutrally, she said, "He must know what he's doing if your father hired him."

Kate scoffed. "My father doesn't know diddly about private investigators."

Rita grinned suddenly. "He certainly was good-looking, don't you think?"

"I really didn't notice," Kate said with elaborate indifference. "He wasn't my type."

Grace wasn't going to touch that with a ten-foot pole. Kate left a few minutes later, but as Grace gave her a goodbye kiss, she couldn't help but wonder if Nick Santos's investigation was going to bring him back to San Francisco in the future. She smiled at the thought. It would be very interesting to see what Kate's reaction would be if he showed up again.

CHAPTER NINE

"WHY ARE YOU SO NERVOUS, Aunt Rita?" Betsy asked on the night they were to see *The Phantom of the Opera* with Erik. They were in the bedroom, and for the third time, Rita had just dropped an earring.

"I'll get it," Betsy said. Her new green-and-red plaid taffeta dress rustled as she bent down and retrieved the earring, which had rolled under the dressing table chair. When she handed the little diamond to her exasperated aunt, she said, "I thought you liked Mr. Mulholland."

Rita took the offending piece of jewelry with a firm grasp so she wouldn't lose it again. "Thank you. And I do like Mr. Mulholland. Furthermore, I'm not nervous, I'm just clumsy tonight." The earring in place, she turned to her niece. "You do look nice, Betsy. So pretty and grown up."

Tomboy Betsy preened and pirouetted so that the petticoats under the skirt made it bell out. They'd gone shopping today, and in addition to the dress, she was wearing new black patent leather pumps and white socks trimmed with the same taffeta as the dress. The outfit had been much too expensive for a child, and Marie was going to kill her, but Rita couldn't resist. And when she saw how proud Betsy was tonight, she was positive that Marie would forgive her and admit it was worth it.

Betsy had also prevailed upon her aunt to braid her unruly mop of hair and wrap it in a coronet around her head. At the last minute, she had even sweet-talked her way into the tiniest dab of lip gloss. Knowing what Marie would say if she knew about *that*, Rita rationalized that this was a special occasion that called for a little bending of the rules. After all, it wasn't every day they were treated to a theater box.

Betsy stopped twirling and grinned saucily at her. "You look nice, too, Aunt Rita. I'm glad you decided to wear that red dress instead of the black."

"Me, too," Rita said, inspecting herself in the mirror. The dress she had finally chosen was more of a wine color than a red, but with four of her discards still tossed across the bed, she was glad she'd decided on something. "Thanks for helping me choose it."

Betsy rolled her big eyes. "It was either that or watch you try on everything in your closet."

Thinking that sometimes this child was much too adult for her tender years, Rita grabbed her beaded evening bag and ushered Betsy downstairs. They had just reached the living room when the doorbell sounded.

"I'll get it!" Betsy shouted.

As the little girl rushed off, Rita stood where she was. Betsy had seen right through her denial about being nervous tonight, so she might as well admit it to herself. She *was* tense. It was ridiculous of her; with a niece in tow, this could hardly be construed as a date. In fact, she could almost consider it an educational outing for Betsy's sake.

Unfortunately, this line of reasoning didn't relax her, either, and she was fussing with her purse when Betsy came back, pulling Erik by the hand.

"Mr. Mulholland said I could call him Uncle Erik," Betsy said. "Is it okay, Aunt Rita?"

Rita looked at the smiling Erik. Her heart sank. He looked so handsome in his dark suit and tie that she wondered if she could refuse him anything.

But the same could be said for her niece, Rita thought, switching her glance to Betsy. She knew how Marie felt about young children addressing adults familiarly, but if Erik had given his okay, she didn't see the harm.

But he wasn't an uncle, or likely to become one, she told herself as she said, "It's up to Erik. Now, fetch your sweater and we'll go."

As the child ran off again, Erik looked at Rita. "I told Betsy how lovely she looked, but you look wonderful, too."

Rita was determined to play it cool tonight. "Thanks," she said. "But before Betsy comes back, I'd also like to thank you again for inviting her tonight. As you can see, she's delighted to be included in such a grown-up event."

"I told you, I was happy to do it."

Their eyes met, and he was about to say something else when Betsy came back into the room. "I'm ready," she announced. "Can we go now?"

To Rita's relief, her talkative niece kept up a running monologue all the way to the theater. Rita did try to stem the flow several times, but Erik seemed more amused than annoyed by the incessant babbling. And as he and Betsy chatted away, she had a chance to calm down and marvel at Erik's unending patience.

Once again, it seemed that she was seeing another side of Erik Mulholland she hadn't known about. These endless surprises, she thought, were a pain in the neck.

Erik had far too many hidden—and fascinating—facets; every time she was sure she had him figured out, he'd do or say something that proved she really didn't know him at all. But what was even more unsettling was the realization that he was a puzzle she wanted to solve.

Forget it, she told herself. They had agreed to a friendship, and that's how it was going to stay. Anything else would make life much too complicated.

KNEELING ON HER CHAIR at the front of the box at stage left, Betsy watched the final act of the musical drama with unwavering attention—as did her aunt. They were the only ones in the box, and Rita was so caught up in the action of the play that she didn't realize for a time that Erik was staring at her instead of at the stage. When she finally felt his gaze on her, she turned to him. Her breath caught. Was she imagining the wealth of emotions she saw in his eyes? In the flickering lights from the stage, his expression made her heart race.

She had to know what he was thinking, so she leaned toward him. "What is it?" she whispered.

On stage, the Phantom was singing of his incredible longing for Christine. As the song swelled, Erik looked at her, seemed about to say something, then shook his head. "It's nothing."

She tried to turn away, but his eyes held her. As he reached for her hand, the powerful music rolled over them, creating a moment of such magical intensity that she felt herself being drawn toward him.

Erik seemed to feel that pull as well. Slowly he lifted his other hand and caressed her cheek. Then he bent toward her. After an exquisite agony of waiting, his lips finally met hers.

It was just a touch, as light as a wisp of air. It couldn't even be truly classified as a kiss, but Rita felt it all the way to her soul. Desire surged to life within her, and she leaned into him. She wanted to forget where she was, or even that her impressionable ten-year-old niece could turn around at any time and see them.

It was this last realization that jerked her back to reality. Trembling, she pulled away. Her heart was hammering; she could hardly breathe. An ache that wouldn't go away throbbed between her thighs, and she had to close her eyes.

Erik let out a ragged breath of his own. When she managed to glance at him, she realized that he'd been just as affected as she by what had just happened. Dazedly, he looked at her and he squeezed her hand. His voice unsteady, he said, "It must be the music."

As she nodded, her head felt as if it were on puppet strings. Somehow she managed to say, "It must be."

But as they turned their attention to the stage again, she knew that the music alone hadn't been responsible for what had just happened. And she was sure that Erik knew it, too. They could deny it all they liked, but something had sprung to life between them again—and had from the moment they'd met in his office with Grace.

So, what now? she wondered. She'd done everything possible to convince herself otherwise, but it was clear that she'd never gotten over her feelings for this man. She'd been so sure that she had banished that intense attraction, or at least learned to control it. It was obvious she'd been fooling herself. How simple it was to say that she no longer felt anything for the man, she thought, when he wasn't around to test her resolve. But the instant he showed up again, the instant he touched her or barely even kissed her, she forgot everything she had so painfully learned.

She didn't *want* to be involved with Erik Mulholland; she didn't want any of this. But it had happened, and now what was she going to do about it?

She was so miserable that she envied the Phantom for being able to disappear, as he did at the end of the show. Blinking, she tried to pull herself together as the lights came up. Fortunately, Betsy's exuberant enthusiasm distracted her, and she was able to make intelligent conversation as they left the theater and walked a short distance for another memento of the evening: an ice cream sundae at one of the nearby restaurants.

Her eyes wide at this unexpected treat, Betsy immediately ordered a gooey chocolate-on-chocolate confection and dug in happily while Rita and Erik sat side by side in the booth, carefully not touching each other. Finally, the excitement of the evening caught up with Betsy, and when she almost nodded off into her melting ice cream, they left the restaurant and walked back to the car. Drowsily, Betsy climbed into the back seat and fell instantly asleep.

On the way home, Erik and Rita were quiet, too. Rita tried to pretend that it was because they were aware of the dozing child, but she knew that wasn't the only reason they didn't speak. She was as aware as Erik was that their brief kiss had changed the dynamics of their relationship—and that now they had to do something about it. They could no longer ignore what was going on between them; it had to be dealt with.

She invited him in for coffee when they got back to her place, and this time he accepted. "You put Betsy to bed," he said. "I'll make it."

Despite the seriousness of her thoughts, Rita couldn't resist teasing him. "Since when do you do anything in the kitchen?"

He smiled. "I've been a lifelong bachelor, remember? I do know how to do a few things for myself."

Of that, she was well aware, she thought. Pointing the way to the kitchen, she led the drowsy child upstairs.

"I want to have coffee, too," Betsy mumbled after Rita helped her change out of her new dress and into her pajamas. Rita smiled.

"Maybe another time, sweetheart," she said, tucking her into bed. "I'll say good-night to Erik for you."

She was almost at the door when Betsy called, "Aunt Rita?"

"Yes, honey?"

"I'm glad you kissed Uncle Erik at the theater."

So she had seen them after all. Wondering what else her sharp-eyed niece had noticed, Rita said firmly, "Good night, Betsy. I'll see you in the morning."

ERIK HAD THE COFFEE MADE by the time she came downstairs again. He'd even found two mugs and was setting them on the counter when she entered the kitchen.

"Let's take it out on the deck," she said. "The view of the bridge at night is really something."

There was no fog on this late-July night, and as they settled in deck chairs, the city lights twinkled far across the bay. A few boats were out, their running lights appearing like fireflies skimming the water. It was a peaceful, beautiful sight that should have been romantic, as well. But now that the moment for the big discussion had arrived, Rita felt even more tense. What was she going to say to Erik? That she found him madly attractive? That she wanted to resume their hot affair? That she'd missed him like crazy and couldn't stand to be apart from him anymore?

In the end, she said nothing. Sipping her coffee, she stared out at the water as though her life depended upon it. And maybe in a way, she thought, it did. Whatever they said now could shape their future. Was she ready for that?

She was beginning to wish that she'd never invited him in when he set aside his mug and said, "Something's going on here, Rita. Do you feel it, too?"

The time had come. But she couldn't just blurt out her feelings for him, so she stood and went to the deck rail. She didn't want to look at him just yet, so she stared out over the black water.

"Yes, I feel it," she said. "I just don't know what to do about it."

She heard him sigh. In relief? Frustration? She didn't have time to decide, for she felt him moving behind her. When she turned, he was there.

"I can't go on pretending," he said. "At first, I thought it was the old attraction leaping up between us—" He hesitated a moment, then went on. "After all, once we were very...physical."

She remembered, only too well. "That's true. But we've been down that road before, Erik, and it's not enough for me. I'm not even sure I want a relationship—with anyone. But if I do get involved, I need more than just a physical attraction."

He turned her toward him. When she looked up, his eyes seemed to sparkle with the reflected lights. "You deserve more, Rita," he said. "It's just that—"

She was sure she knew what he was going to say. A chill settled over her despite the warm night, and she pulled away from him. "I see," she said. "You're attracted to me, and you'd like to take up where we left off, but you just don't feel you can ask. Is that right? Well, I've heard this story before. That's what you told me—"

"I was a fool then." His eyes never left hers. "A fool," he repeated. "I never should have let you go...."

The icy feeling that had wrapped around her only moments before vanished in the heat of his body as he moved toward her. As though she had no will of her own, she allowed him to put his hands on her arms and draw her closer. She knew he was going to kiss her, and she knew, too, that this time the kiss wouldn't be a brief, light caress as before. She didn't care; she couldn't fight it any longer. If this was going to be, it was going to be. Lifting her arms, she drew his mouth down to hers.

The contact of their mouths, their tongues, their bodies rocked them both. Lost in immediate sensation, she clung fiercely to him. For a crazy moment, she thought the deck was tilting beneath her feet.

"Oh, Rita," he whispered.

His arms went around her and he pulled her so tightly into him that she could feel the hard pounding of his heart against her chest. Her own pulse bounded in response, and she reached up and grabbed a handful of his thick hair. Her dress was low-cut in back, and when he touched her bare skin, her knees threatened to buckle from the contact. *It's been so long!* she thought. *So long!*

He raised his head for a moment. His voice hoarse, he whispered, "Let's go inside...."

More than anything in the world, she wanted to make love to him. She longed to feel his naked body next to hers; she yearned for his touch on her bare skin. She wanted to straddle him and see the wonder on his face; she wanted to look up at him and marvel at how perfectly they fit together, how they moved together as one.

But then she thought of something and pulled back. "We can't," she said. "Betsy—"

"Betsy's asleep," he whispered. He kissed her again, so deeply that she wanted to make love to him right there. Gasping, she managed to move away a second time.

"I can't," she said miserably. "It wouldn't be right. Not with my niece in the house..."

He didn't say anything for a long few seconds. Sure she had ruined it all, she wondered what she would do if he just turned and walked out on her. Finally, she risked a quick glance at his face, expecting...she didn't know what. To her relief, he looked as unhappy as she felt. She touched his arm.

"I'm sorry, Erik."

"So am I," he said with a heavy sigh. "But then, maybe it wouldn't have been a good idea, anyway."

"What do you mean?"

He hesitated a moment. "There's something I haven't told you."

"Oh?" she said, trying to remain calm. She definitely didn't like the sound of *that*.

He winced. "I'm going to tell you something, and I don't want you to be angry—"

She hated it when someone told her not to get angry. Already she could feel herself getting steamed, and she didn't even know what he was going to say.

"Why would I get angry?" she asked tightly.

"Because the truth is, I've been seeing someone."

Seeing someone? What exactly did that mean? She felt a sharp stab of resentment, but then she wondered what she had expected. Was it reasonable to think that he'd been a monk this past year? Of course he was seeing someone. She frowned. Knowing him, he was probably seeing quite a few someones.

"I see," she said.

He didn't like her tone. "I know what you're thinking—"

"Do you? That's interesting. Because at the moment, *I* don't know what I'm thinking. But never mind. Before we go on with this, I want to ask you something."

"Anything," he said. "What is it?"

"Just how serious is this relationship you mentioned?"

When he glanced away, she knew she had her answer. Anger flooded through her after all, and she despised herself for falling for his act a second time. Hadn't she learned anything from past experience?

It seemed not. When she remembered how ardent she'd been only moments ago, she felt so mortified she wanted to jump into the bay. How could she have been so eager to go inside, so anxious to take him up to her bedroom and make passionate love with him? The thought that he was seriously seeing someone made her writhe. What was the matter with her? Had she lost all dignity?

Apparently so. But this was the end of it. Since she had to, she'd work with him; if necessary, she'd see him every day until the store was up and running. But that was all. She would not get involved with a man who could kiss her as he had just now, when he was committed to someone else.

"I think you'd better go, Erik," she said coldly. "Obviously, as it was before, this has been a mistake. A *big* mistake."

"Wait, Rita. You don't understand."

"Yes, I do. I understand that you're a two-timing—"

"No, I'm not. Please listen." He reached for her, but she gave him a look that stopped him in midgesture. He dropped his hand to his side. "I didn't expect to develop these…these feelings for you. That's the last thing I wanted, believe me."

She stiffened. "Thank you so much!"

"I didn't mean it like that, and you know it. In fact, I'm willing to bet that you didn't want to have any feelings for me, either."

"Well, that's not *quite* true, Erik. I was perfectly content despising you all these months."

He grimaced, but went on. "Look, we both know that things have changed between us—"

"You got that right!"

"I meant, before this conversation."

She was being childish and she knew it. Tightening her lips, she said, "All right. Go on."

"As I said, I didn't mean for this to happen, but it has. Now we have to deal with it."

"We don't have to *deal* with anything. You're involved with someone. You just told me that. End of story. Fini. Kaput."

"No, it's not the end. At least, I don't want it to be."

"Oh, so you want to continue seeing *both* of us, is that it?"

"No. Even before we met again, I was having second thoughts about Caroline."

Now she had a name. *Caroline*. She bet he called her that, too. Not Caro or Carrie, but *Caroline*. She had always liked that name, but she hated it now.

"And when did these second thoughts begin, Erik? Before or after you decided you wanted to go to bed with me again?"

"You're not being fair," he said quietly. "I was going to tell you about her."

"When?"

He winced again at that—as well he might, she thought angrily. Just when *had* he intended to mention this other woman?

"Can I explain?" he asked.

She crossed her arms. "You can try."

"I met her a while ago at a fund-raiser. I thought..." He stopped. "Damn it, this is really awkward."

She looked at him frostily. "I couldn't agree more. But it's your own fault. *I'm* not the one who's involved with someone, *you* are."

"That's what I'm trying to tell you," he said. "I won't be involved for long."

She wasn't going to let him get away with that. "Oh, really? I see. You're going to throw *her* over now."

"It's not like that. Even before you and I met, I'd begun to question my relationship with Caroline. I admit that at one time I thought I wanted to marry her—"

"*Marry* her!"

"I never asked her," he said hastily. "Rudy always said she wasn't the right woman for me, and he was right."

"So now what?"

"Now I'm going to tell her that I can't see her anymore."

"And what is she going to have to say about *that?*"

"I don't know. She probably won't like it. But it wouldn't be fair to continue seeing her, when all I want to do is see you."

She didn't know what to say to that. Not sure how she felt, she turned away from him and stared out at the water. What did she want? A part of her still yearned for his touch, the look in his eyes, his laugh. But another part of her held back. She couldn't bear the hurt if she agreed to try a second time with him and it didn't work out. It had taken her months to get over him the first time. She wouldn't put herself through that again.

"Rita?"

She wouldn't look at him. "I don't know, Erik," she said. "Maybe . . ."

He put his hands lightly on her shoulders, and she tensed but found she couldn't move away. Obviously encouraged that she hadn't rejected him outright, he tightened his grip slightly. His body was like a big, solid wall behind her, and it was tempting just to lean back into him and pretend that everything would work out. She made herself stand where she was.

"No matter what you decide," he said softly, "I'm still going to tell Caroline that it's all over."

She closed her eyes. "When are you going to tell her?"

"Tomorrow."

"Are you just saying this to—"

He turned her toward him. "I mean it, Rita. I want us to continue seeing each other. But first I have to break it off with her. And I will."

She wanted to believe him. But she had trusted him before, and he had betrayed her. Now she didn't know what was right. Things had been so much easier when she hated him, she thought. But how could she hate a man who, among other things, had given her niece such a wonderful night? Without wanting to, she thought of him helping a sleepy Betsy from the car after they got home tonight. He'd been so patient, so gentle, and Betsy had been delighted at all the attention. It hadn't been an act, either, Rita knew. A child could sense a phony a mile away.

This wasn't the Erik she remembered from the past. Maybe, as he insisted, he really had changed. And if that were so, didn't she owe him the opportunity to prove it to her?

She wondered if she was just rationalizing. Maybe she didn't *want* to separate fact from fantasy. But he was waiting for her to say something, so she said, "All right, Erik. After you tell her, we'll . . . see."

It clearly wasn't as much as he'd hoped for, but he didn't argue. He left soon after, and even though she was exhausted, it was a long time before she slept that night.

Had she done the right thing? she wondered again and again. It was too late now. The only thing she could do was to wait and see if she'd been a fool the second time around.

CHAPTER TEN

"FOR HEAVEN'S SAKE, Jeffrey," Grace said into the telephone. This was the first time she'd spoken to her husband since Nick Santos had shown up, and she was trying to control her temper and her patience. "You could have warned me, you know. I hardly knew what to say when that detective appeared on the doorstep."

Jeffrey was being his officious best, pointing out, "I did send you a memo, Grace."

He knew that pedantic manner drove her wild. To give him a taste of his own medicine, she said coolly, "I detest memos, as you're very well aware. I realize things are a little...strained between us at the moment, but don't you think you could have given me the courtesy of a telephone call?"

He didn't care for her tone, either. Just as stiffly, he said, "I didn't know when Mr. Santos would arrive."

"While *I* didn't even know he existed."

Abruptly, she realized that tit-for-tat wasn't productive at all. Rubbing her temple, where she could feel a headache coming on, she said, "All right, let's not argue about it anymore. What's done is done. It's just that the man took me by surprise."

"We were all surprised. When that tiara showed up in New York...well, you can imagine what we all thought."

Grace could indeed. The theft of six pieces from the world famous DeWilde collection had been a carefully guarded secret, but now that one of the jewels had appeared, the pretense had been shattered. If word got out, questions were bound to be raised.

Which was why Jeffrey had hired a private investigator. Grace understood that. What she couldn't understand was why he hadn't warned her that Nick Santos would arrive to question her.

"I still think you should have told me," she said severely. "I know how your family values privacy, Jeffrey, but it was unsettling enough to find out that a piece of the collection had suddenly surfaced. To be unexpectedly confronted by an investigator was almost as disturbing. At first I wasn't even sure he was legitimate."

"I'm certain he had identification. And he did carry a letter from me."

"Both of which could be easily forged, if he was up to no good."

Jeffrey sighed. "This isn't really about the investigator, is it, Grace?"

"Well, of course it—" Grace stopped. Irritated that he seemed to have seen through her, she felt she had no choice but to admit, "No, you're right. It isn't."

"Then what?"

There were so many things, she thought. But she settled on one that was uppermost in her mind. "The truth is, I'm so *tired* of fighting about every detail regarding this reception we're supposed to be giving for Gabe and Lianne."

"It's not my fault that you're half a world away and that you're so damned busy with—"

"Don't say it," she warned. "You've made it crystal clear how you feel about my opening a store."

"Ah, now we've really come to the crux of the problem, haven't we."

"Have we? You have no right to try and stop me, Jeffrey. I'm not competing with you in any way."

"The board sees it differently."

"And how do *you* see it?"

"Haven't we got off track here?" he parried. "I thought the purpose of this call was to discuss the investigation by Mr. Santos. I'd like to know if we can count on your cooperation."

He'd shut her off again—as he had ever since that horrible night when everything began to go wrong. Frustrated and angry, she snapped, "No, you cannot count on my cooperation. As I told Mr. Santos, I don't know anything about those jewels. And to tell you the truth, I could care less. I have my own concerns at the moment."

"A fact that you've made painfully obvious. But I caution you to remember one thing—"

"And that is?"

"The corporation will do everything necessary to protect itself."

By this time she was so irritated that she said, "Well, fine, Jeffrey. At least we're on the same wavelength about one thing. Because I assure you, I'll do everything I can to guard my own interests."

Exasperated, she broke the connection. Not even a cup of tea restored her equilibrium, and she was still fuming an hour later when Rita came in. She didn't want to subject her assistant to her foul mood, so she excused her bad humor by saying she had a headache and suggesting they get right down to work.

"AND SO THE CONTRACTOR CALLED and said that...Grace? You seem so preoccupied. Is anything wrong?"

Grace started guiltily. It was midmorning by this time, and she was still distracted. When she saw Rita's concern, she said, "I'm sorry. I guess I am a little perturbed."

"Do you still have your headache? I can run out and get something for it."

"You're a dear, but no thank you. I'm afraid it's just tension. I talked to Jeffrey this morning, and though I had intended to discuss the reception for Gabriel and Lianne, we got completely off track and into something else."

"I am sorry."

Grace sighed. "I'm sorry, too—about so many things. I'd thought that since we couldn't have a wedding, at least we could celebrate after the fact. But Jeffrey and I can't seem to agree on anything. Now we have to deal with a private investigator poking into our lives."

"I sympathize. I wouldn't like someone delving into my family's private affairs."

"Well, it does feel so...tawdry," Grace said. She thought of Nick Santos and had to add, "Still, if it has to be done, Mr. Santos seems competent enough."

Rita smiled. "I don't think Kate liked him very much."

When she remembered the meeting between the big investigator and her difficult youngest child, Grace smiled, too. "No, but we can't judge the poor man by that. Kate is my daughter, and I love her dearly, but she can be judgmental at times."

"Maybe she was just taken by surprise, too. Having someone like that show up out of the blue is an unnerving experience."

Despite Jeffrey's insistence that this remain strictly a family matter, Grace decided that Rita had to know a few details—if only to help deflect what she suspected would be inevitable publicity. The appearance of the DeWilde tiara would make too good a tale for some intrepid reporter to miss, and she wanted to be prepared. They had to know what to say—and what not to.

"I've been meaning to discuss this business with you, Rita," she began slowly. "I know that you'll be discreet, but just in case someone hears the tale and calls asking for details, we have to have our story straight." She paused for a moment, collecting her thoughts. Then she said, "Do you know anything about the DeWilde jewels?"

"Just that every piece has a history," Rita replied.

"Indeed, they do. In fact, one of the pieces was supposedly worn by the Empress Eugénie of France on the occasion of her wedding to Louis-Napoléon—Napoléon III."

Rita looked impressed. "Good heavens, I had no idea."

Grace smiled. "Even the descriptions of the jewels are enough to tantalize the imagination. One piece is called a 'dancing waters' necklace and contains sapphires and white intricately cut diamonds. Another is a double-rose brooch of rubies, diamonds, emeralds and black onyx. Then, of course, there are the earrings of diamonds and Burmese rubies."

"They all sound fabulous."

"Oh, they are. But remember, the DeWilde family tree is filled with jewelers. In fact, the business began with Maximilien DeWilde, who was apprenticed to a diamond merchant in Amsterdam. He married the daughter of one of his jewelry-makers who bought un- cut diamonds, and their daughter, Marie, became a de- signer herself. Their son, Mâx, started out in watch repair, but later operated an exclusive jewelry shop called DeWilde's. So you see, there is quite a history here.''

Rita was sitting on the couch, opposite Grace. She leaned forward, her face alight. ''Tell me more.''

''Well, let me think. Oh, yes... Max's sister, Marie, never married but became a famous designer who spe- cialized in jeweled evening bags and other fabulous pieces. Then, later, she joined with her brother and his wife, Genevieve, and expanded Max's shop into an ex- clusive small department store. When they incorpo- rated her jewelry and accessories into a boutique within the store, the modern DeWilde's was born.''

''What a story,'' Rita breathed. ''It could be a book.''

''Oh, I doubt that will happen,'' Grace said with a laugh. Suddenly, she sobered. ''Still, now that the tiara has appeared, I wonder what else—if anything—might be next.''

Rita and Grace spent the rest of the day immersed in numerous details about the store, and Rita lost track of time. Almost before she knew it, the clock chimed six, and Grace stood and rubbed her neck.

''I don't know about you,'' she said, ''but I've had it for the day. Let's quit for now and start again tomor- row.''

''That's fine with me.'' Rita was tired, too. She was gathering file folders and brochures to stuff into her briefcase, when Grace asked her what she was doing.

"I thought I'd get some studying in," Rita said. "There's so much I need to learn."

"But you're always working. Don't you ever take a night off?"

"All the time," Rita insisted, although it wasn't quite true. "I went to see *The Phantom of the Opera* on Saturday night, didn't I?"

"Ah, yes, so you did. You and Erik took your niece, is that right?"

"Yes, and she was over the moon at being included. We had a box, and I have to admit it was wonderful."

"Erik told me that he enjoyed himself as well."

"He did? When?"

"He mentioned it the other day when he called. In fact, he sounded quite pleased to have escorted—and these are his words—'two lovely ladies' to the theater."

Rita hadn't heard from Erik since Saturday night. It was now Tuesday, and she was trying to remain calm when what she wanted to do was explode. When he'd told her the other night that he would talk to Caroline soon, she'd believed him. But it was days later, and there'd been no word. She was beginning to think that he'd changed his mind.

Which was just fine with her, she thought resentfully after she'd said good-night to Grace and was on her way home. If Erik wasn't going to break off his relationship with "the other woman," then she was better off by herself. She'd been getting along quite well without Erik Mulholland in her life, thank you very much.

Still, it hurt. Despite the odds, she'd been so hopeful this time. What a fool she was. Why couldn't she just accept that she and Erik weren't meant to be?

She arrived home and parked the car. But after she'd unlocked the front door, she couldn't stop herself from immediately glancing at the answering machine. It was on the mail table in the foyer, and when she saw no red light glowing to indicate that she had a message, she was furious with herself. If she really believed that things had worked out for the best, why did she still care if Erik called or not?

"I don't," she said firmly, and closed the front door with a kick.

ERIK HADN'T CALLED because he was still trying to have that talk with Caroline. To phone her with the news that he'd decided not to see her anymore seemed callous and cold, but every time he had attempted to see her in person, something prevented him. If it wasn't his business, it was a conflict with her schedule.

Finally, all too aware that he hadn't spoken to Rita in days, he had to insist to Caroline that they meet.

"Well, of course, darling," she'd said at once. "I didn't realize it was so important." She lowered her voice, almost purring the words. "Do I dare assume—"

He didn't want her to think that he'd made a decision about the vice presidency with Morton, Madison and Shade; it would be even worse if she thought that he'd finally dredged up enough courage to propose. Hastily, he said, "I'd rather talk about it when I see you."

"In that case, how about tonight?"

They agreed to go out for dinner. He was eager to call Rita, so as soon as he hung up with Caroline, he immediately reached for the phone again. Then he changed his mind. He had already promised himself that he wouldn't contact Rita until he had completely broken off all ties with Caroline. Now that he and Rita might have a second chance, he wanted to begin with a clean slate. He didn't want any misconceptions or disputes to mar their relationship this time. He'd wait until he told Caroline what he had decided. Then, he'd call.

As soon as Caroline opened the door that night, Erik knew things weren't going to go well. For starters, she'd answered the bell herself instead of allowing one of the servants to do it, and instead of being dressed to go out, she was wearing an outfit he knew she'd never wear in public. It consisted of a long split skirt and a jeweled blouse, both of some filmy material. Obviously, she had changed their plans.

"Darling!" she exclaimed, throwing herself into his arms. "Oh, have I a surprise for you!"

He was already surprised enough. Gingerly extricating himself from her embrace, he held her at arm's length and said, "You look . . . so different, Caroline. I don't believe I've . . . er . . . ever seen you wearing something like this."

Delighted that he had noticed, she pirouetted in front of him. The wide legs of her nearly transparent culottes ballooned out, providing him with a startling— and, he had to admit, provocative—glimpse of a shapely leg.

"Do you like it?" she asked, coming back to stand in front of him. He was wearing the suit he'd worn to the office, and she put her hands on his chest, running her fingers up under the lapels of his jacket. The gesture was so unlike her—so *seductive*—that he quickly grabbed her hands.

"Yes, I like it," he said. He knew he had to get control of this situation in a hurry before it got even more out of hand. "But, Caroline—"

"I'm so glad," she whispered, "because I bought it just for you." She lowered her voice even more. "Just for tonight..."

"Caroline, we have to talk—"

"Yes," she said, "we certainly do."

She took his hands and began to pull him toward the study. "Mother and Daddy are out for the evening, and I've had the servants put up a table just for us. We'll be all alone, and we can talk about whatever we want to."

Erik didn't want to hurt her feelings, but he knew he couldn't keep up the pretense through an entire meal. He was already edgy, and no matter how much trouble she had taken tonight, he had to tell her now.

"Let's go into the living room for a minute," he said.

She turned to look at him, a puzzled frown between her perfectly sculpted eyebrows. "The living room? But why?"

"Well, we can...talk better in there."

"But—" She stopped when she saw his expression, and a change came over her face. "What is this about, Erik?"

He wasn't going to tell her while they were standing in the hall. The door to the living room was to his right, and he pulled her inside. He hadn't planned on doing it this way, but he seemed to have no choice. "I didn't want to tell you this so baldly, Caroline, but...we can't see each other anymore."

She just looked at him. Finally, she said, "I beg your pardon?"

He was beginning to wish that he'd phoned—or better yet, just sent a note. But he led her to one of the living room couches and gently pressed her down. He sat beside her and reached for one of her hands.

"I know this might be hard to understand, Caroline," he said, "but the truth is..." He took a deep breath. "I've met someone."

Again, she just looked at him. Her blank stare was unnerving, and he was wondering if he should say more, or just leave things alone, when she said, "*Someone.* Who is she, Erik?"

"Does it matter?" He didn't want to get into this. "I don't think it's necessary for us to—"

Right before his eyes, her face changed. The glazed look in her eyes was quickly replaced by such a furious expression that he was taken aback. He'd never seen her like this, and before he could think of anything to say, she shot to her feet. He automatically stood, too.

Her voice was shaking with anger when she spoke. "How *dare* you try to tell me it doesn't matter! Of course it matters! Who is she, Erik? I want to know!"

He wanted to get past this damned preoccupation with Rita's identity. Hoping to quiet her enough so that the servants wouldn't hear and wonder what was going on, he said, "Her name is Rita Shannon. But—"

"When did you meet her? How? Where?"

"She's someone I knew...a while ago."

"Someone you knew. A while ago. Well, how very convenient for you."

"Caroline, will you please calm down?"

"I *am* calm!" she stormed. Angry comprehension dawned in her eyes. "You wanted to marry her, didn't you?"

"I don't know. We didn't discuss it then."

"And you have discussed it now?"

"No! We haven't discussed anything. But it doesn't matter, Caroline. The point is—"

"Oh, I know what the point is! Whoever she is, this woman thinks she's going to ruin all my wonderful plans—not to mention my entire future!"

He made the mistake of saying, "I know how you must feel, and I'm sorry, but—"

Her eyes blazed. "You're *sorry?* Oh, you don't know the meaning of sorry!"

Was she threatening him? No, he wouldn't believe it; she was just upset. He couldn't blame her. If he'd been in her position, he'd be upset, too. He felt guilty at the way this was turning out, but then he reminded himself that he'd never made any promises to her, verbal or otherwise.

Thank God he hadn't proposed, he thought, and said, "I think I'd better go."

"Oh, no, you don't! You're not going until we settle this!"

"We have settled it. I told you I was sorry, and you're just going to have to understand—"

"Oh, I understand all right, Erik. And now you're going to apologize and tell me that this was all just a joke in terribly bad taste!"

He was sure he hadn't heard right. "What?"

"Do I have to repeat myself? Very well, I will. I want you to tell me that you've made a mistake. That you're not involved with this . . . this woman, and that *I'm* the one you really love. Then we can go into dinner and have the evening I so carefully planned."

He stared at her. Was she out of her mind?

"That's not possible," he finally said. "I came here tonight to tell you that I can't see you anymore. You're going to have to accept it."

"No, I don't think so, Erik. Because you see, I'm not going to let you go without a fight."

"A fight? What are you talking about?"

Gone was the adoring woman he'd known; in her place was a spoiled, arrogant creature accustomed to getting her own way. He'd seen glimpses of this true persona before, but until tonight she had always been careful not to show him too much. Now he saw it all. And what he saw, he didn't like.

"You let me believe that you intended to propose, Erik," she said, her voice hard. "You allowed me to think that we were going to be married—"

He stiffened. "I never said—"

"Oh, yes, you did. You distinctly made me a verbal promise. And I intend to hold you to it."

He'd managed not to lose his temper throughout this increasingly bizarre conversation, but he was perilously close to losing it now. Tightly, he said, "You can't hold me to anything, Caroline. I never promised you marriage, and you know it."

"Do I? Well, think about this, Erik. If push comes to shove, which one of us do you think people will believe?"

He was incredulous. "You can't be serious!"

"Indeed I am. Just like you were when you told me you wanted me to be your wife."

"I can't believe this!"

"Believe it," she said tautly. "Because, one way or another, I intend for us to be married."

All he wanted to do was get out of here and never come back. "Then I feel sorry for you, Caroline. Because this time, no matter how much you might want it, it just isn't going to be."

She saw him to the door; she stared confidently after him when he drove away. He knew she did, because he watched her in the rearview mirror. He shook his head, glad when he turned the corner and she disappeared from sight. He let out the breath he'd been unconsciously holding, and by sheer effort managed to ease his viselike grip on the steering wheel. If he didn't know better, he thought, he might have believed he'd dreamed that whole nightmare scene.

She didn't mean it, he told himself, thinking of Caroline again after he'd arrived home and made a beeline for the bar. He had intended on calling Rita as soon as he got here to tell her the deed was done, but he needed a drink first.

As the ice cubes clattered into the glass, he tried again to convince himself that Caroline had been attempting to salvage her dignity. She'd been hurt and upset, but tomorrow—or the next day, or the next—she'd realize how empty her threat was to force him to marry her, and bow out gracefully.

But would she?

Of course she would, he assured himself. But perhaps he wasn't quite as certain as he pretended, for he never did call Rita that night. And it was a long time before he finally fell into an uneasy sleep.

CHAPTER ELEVEN

RITA WAS AT WORK on Wednesday morning when Erik finally called. She'd spent the sleepless nights since their last meeting thinking about the situation and wondering how she'd react when she heard his voice. She found out at once. With the first word he spoke, she became angry. She almost hung up on him, but then she decided it would be infinitely more satisfying to give him a piece of her mind.

"Well, well," she said. "How very nice of you to call."

It was impossible to miss her sarcasm. "Now, Rita, I know you're upset."

"Upset? Whatever makes you think that, Erik? Just because you promised to call days ago and never got around to it doesn't mean I'm angry. I should have known you'd have so many other *important* things to do."

"I can explain."

"Really? No, I don't think so. Once again you have proved yourself to be the man I always knew you were. But guess what? I'm actually relieved. I thought I'd made a mistake last year, judging you so harshly..." Despite herself, her voice rose. "But now I realize that I had you pegged all along. Don't call me again on a personal note, Erik. In fact, if we weren't both working for Grace, I'd tell you that I never wanted to speak to you or to see you ever again. Have I made myself clear?''

''As crystal,'' he said. ''But if you'd just—''

She hung up on him.

An hour later, the first bouquet of roses arrived. She knew who it was from, and she tore up the card without even reading it. She would have thrown the flowers in the trash, except that she would have had to explain what they were doing there to Grace. Her face set, she found a vase in the kitchen, but just to be perverse, she didn't add water. The sight of the beautiful bouquet made her furious all over again, and she smashed the stems into the crystal, poking herself with a missed thorn in the process.

''Well, *that* figures!'' she exclaimed angrily when she saw the bright red drop of blood welling up on her thumb. It was tempting to throw the whole thing out the window, but just in time she remembered Grace and put the disheveled, forlorn-looking bouquet on the counter instead. That didn't stop her from giving it a glare as she left the room and stormed back to her desk.

If Erik really believed a few roses made up for his appalling lack of consideration, he could think again. At this point, she didn't even care if he *had* told Caroline he wasn't going to see her anymore. In fact, she thought in a temper, maybe she should give the woman a call herself and ask her out for a drink. They could commiserate about what a rat Erik Mulholland was.

''Flowers!'' Grace said when she came in. Then she took a closer look at the broken stems and the crushed petals and asked, ''What happened to them?''

Rita had her explanation ready. ''I got them from a street vendor,'' she lied. ''He came over to the car when

I was at a stop light and wouldn't get out of my way until I bought some.''

"I see." Grace peered at the vase. "Er...don't you think they need a little water?''

Rita was about to reply when the doorbell rang. When she answered it, she was greeted by another bouquet, this one twice as big and even more difficult to hide. Grimly she told the delivery person, "I'm sorry, but you've got the wrong address.''

"Oh, I don't think so," the girl said earnestly. "See here? It says—''

Accepting the flowers, Rita thanked her and shut the door. She realized Grace was looking at her curiously, and she sighed. "All right, I lied." Although she knew who these were from, too, she glanced at the envelope tucked into the ferns. The sight of Erik's bold signature irritated her even more, and her voice was clipped as she explained, "Those other flowers were from Erik. So are these. Would you like them?''

She thrust the huge bouquet toward Grace, who looked surprised as she gathered it into her arms. "My, my," Grace said. "Aren't you even going to read the card?''

"No. I don't care what it says," Rita told her. She tore this one up, too, and threw it in the wastebasket. Dusting off her hands, she went to her desk and sat down. "Now I can get back to work.''

An hour later, the doorbell rang again. This time, Grace said hastily, "I'll get it.''

She returned with yet another bouquet, this one holding at least three dozen red roses. Hesitantly, she looked at Rita, who was furiously drumming her pen against the top of her desk.

"I take it," Grace said, "that you don't want these, either?"

Rita didn't even glance at the froth of baby's breath and other greenery surrounding the perfect blooms. "No, I don't. I don't want anything from that man."

"Rita, dear, I realize it's none of my business, but obviously there's been a...problem between you and Erik. Now, it seems to me that he's at least *trying* to make amends. Don't you think you could hear him out?"

"No," Rita said stubbornly. "I don't care what he has to say. It doesn't matter to me anymore."

Grace didn't argue. Sighing, she went off to the kitchen to locate a big enough container to hold this arrangement. Her mouth tight, Rita went back to work.

The doorbell rang again a scant forty-five minutes later. "For heaven's sake!" Rita exclaimed. "Why can't the man get the hint?"

"I'll get it," Grace said again, but Rita held up her hand.

"No, I'll answer. And *this* time, I'm going to tell the florist I won't accept any more bouquets, under *any* circumstances. They can deliver them to hospitals or convalescent homes, I don't care. This has gone far enough."

She jerked the door open. "Now, listen—" she started to say.

It wasn't the girl who had delivered the first three bouquets. Almost hidden behind four dozen roses, Erik was standing outside. When she saw him, she immediately demanded, "What are you doing here?"

He peered out from behind the immense bouquet. "I figured that when I didn't get any response to my other efforts, you were probably going to kill the messenger on the fourth try. So instead of putting the delivery person at risk, I decided I'd better come myself."

"Very funny," she said. She kept hold of the door so he couldn't get by her. "What do you want?"

"Er... do you think I could come in?"

"No. If you want to say something, you can say it out there. But please hurry. This is a place of business, and I have a lot of work to do."

Erik sighed. "You're a hard woman, Rita Shannon."

She didn't deign to answer—or to argue.

"It wasn't my fault, Rita."

She couldn't resist. "No? What went wrong? Did you break your arm so you couldn't pick up the phone?"

"I told you I wanted to talk to Caroline in person before I called you."

"And you're both such social butterflies that you just couldn't get together. I understand, Erik. Now, go away."

"I did finally speak to her."

"Good for you." She began to shut the door.

He stuck the flowers in so she couldn't close it all the way. "Wait, Rita, please."

"No. We have nothing more to say to each other. If talking to Caroline was really important to you, you would have managed it a lot sooner."

"You're right," he said. "The delay was inexcusable, and I don't blame you for being angry with me, because you have every right to feel the way you do. But I'd like to think there's a way to get past this. Please tell me there is. I can't bear the thought that we've come this far, only to throw it away because of a stupid error on my part."

She had never heard him talk this way, and it gave her pause. She wanted to believe him, but was this just another excuse? She looked at him suspiciously.

"What did you tell her?" she asked.

"I told her I couldn't see her anymore."

"And?"

"And . . . we're not seeing each other."

She was silent. Wasn't this what she'd wanted, what she'd asked of him? What more did she expect him to do? Cautiously, she opened the door an inch more.

"Just like that?" she asked.

He looked uncomfortable. "Well, it wasn't quite that easy. Caroline was a little . . . upset."

"And what did you do about that?"

"I told her I was sorry, but it couldn't be helped."

"And she said?"

"Look, does it matter? Isn't the important thing that I'm not seeing her now? Please, Rita, I know I should have called you sooner, but I just didn't think it would be fair to Caroline—or to you—until I got this other thing straightened out. I'm sorry it took so long. But now it's done. Can't we move on from here?"

He was saying all the right things, so why did she sense there was more to it than what he was telling her? Maybe she was being too distrustful, she thought, and opened the door another inch.

"I'm not sure," she said. "Maybe this was a mistake after all."

"Do you really believe that?"

"I don't know what to believe."

Quickly, he pressed what little advantage he had. "Why don't we go to dinner tonight and talk about it?"

"I'm not sure that's a good idea."

"Yes, it is, you know it is. I do want to see you, Rita. Please say yes."

With their history, she knew the smartest thing she could have done was to tell him that she'd changed her mind and had decided that dating him wasn't such a good idea after all. This latest incident gave her the perfect excuse. All she had to do was take it.

Instead, she said, "Well . . . maybe a dinner wouldn't hurt."

He smiled at her less-than-enthusiastic acceptance. But after negotiating his way out of a sticky situation, he wasn't going to question it. "Good," he said. "You can come to my place."

"You're going to cook?"

He felt confident enough to tease her. "Unlike you, I know my way around a kitchen."

"Big deal," she scoffed. "You made the coffee the other night."

"I'll do a lot more tonight. So, is it a date?"

She knew she should refuse, but how could she when he was looking at her like that? He smiled tentatively, and she found herself smiling faintly back.

"All right," she said reluctantly, still not sure she was doing the right thing. "It's a date."

He broke into a broad grin. "That's great."

She wanted to keep her mind on mundane details, so she asked, "What time, and what can I bring?"

"How about eight o'clock? And just bring yourself."

It was that grin of his that won her over. Trying not to smile herself, she said, "No takeout, just in case?"

"No, let's just live dangerously."

On semisolid ground now, he gently pushed the door all the way open, handed her the flowers, gave her a quick kiss on the lips and left.

Grace returned from the kitchen as Rita closed the door. She was carrying the largest vase she had, and she gestured toward the roses Rita was holding.

"I hope this is the last," she said with a smile, "because I've just run out of vases."

ON THE WAY TO ERIK'S apartment for dinner that night, Rita remembered the throwaway comment he'd made about living dangerously. She had smiled about it at the time, but the truth was, where he was concerned, she *was* living on the edge. No matter how attracted she was to him, no matter how much he seemed to have changed since the last time, getting involved with him again seemed to be asking for trouble. Did she really know what she was doing?

No, she thought. But then, she had always led with her heart instead of her head. It was a major character flaw, she felt, but no matter how she tried to correct it, she failed.

But it will be different this time, she told herself. She and Erik were both older and wiser. They'd learned a lot from their previous experience, and they wouldn't repeat the same mistakes.

Besides, she thought, this time Erik was being honest. He'd told her he was in a relationship with someone else, he had promised to break it off, and he had. A little late, but he'd finally managed it. She couldn't ask for more; he'd done everything she wanted.

So why did she feel so uneasy? Suspicion wasn't normally part of her nature, and she hated assigning nefarious motives to things people said or did. She and

Erik would never develop a real relationship if she continued to mistrust him, so it seemed she either had to forgive him completely or break it off now, before things became even more complicated. Which was it to be?

She was still dithering when she turned onto Erik's street. But as she parked the car in front of his condo, she decided that maybe she was making too big a deal out of nothing. After all, they weren't getting *married* tonight; all they were doing was having dinner. And nowhere, she thought, was it written that a meal had to lead to anything else.

Erik answered the door before the chimes stopped ringing. He was wearing slacks and a sport shirt, but had embellished his outfit with a frilly apron tied around his waist. She had to laugh.

"Now, that's what I like to see," she said. "A man who knows his place."

With a flourish he took the chardonnay she'd brought, and before she realized what he was going to do, he swept her into his house and into his arms. But instead of the deep, passionate embrace she had almost expected—had envisioned and wanted, in fact—he quickly kissed the tip of her nose and released her.

"Gotta get back to the stove," he said. "Would you like a drink?"

"No, I'll wait for the wine at dinner," she said, although she was tempted to accept his offer. That all-too-brief interlude in his arms had been disconcerting, and she wondered how she was going to get through dinner if a simple gesture like that had such power over her.

"Suit yourself," he said. "I've got some hors d'oeuvres, if you like."

She followed as he headed off to the kitchen. She'd been here before when they were involved, but as with his office, he'd redecorated. She had to admit that she liked it. Pale beige carpet flowed from the living room to the edge of the dining room, whose new hardwood floor had been buffed to a high gloss. Huge modern paintings hung on dark apricot walls; couches and chairs predominated in tones of golds and greens. The color scheme was masculine and restful at the same time, and she thought it suited him perfectly.

The kitchen had been redone, too, she noted. Instead of stark white, it had been painted a cream color, and the brown tile countertops had been replaced by smooth ebony ones. Although the major appliances were also black, colorful copper pans hung over the stove, providing contrast. Erik was tossing the salad when she came in, and he smiled when he saw her expression.

"Like it?" he asked.

"It's wonderful," she said honestly. "Who's your decorator?"

She hadn't meant to ask that; as soon as the words were out of her mouth, she almost expected him to say that Caroline had been the one. But instead he said, "I didn't have a decorator. I did it myself."

"In that case, maybe you should go into the business," she teased. "I could recommend you to my entire family. They'd keep you busy for a while."

"Thanks, but no," he said. "I did it once, and that's enough for a lifetime. But go take a look outside. One thing I finally did do was to have the whirlpool spa put in."

She hadn't checked out the minuscule backyard yet. But when he mentioned the whirlpool, she immediately remembered past discussions about it. They had planned where it would go—and what they would do with it after it was installed. There was supposed to be something incredibly erotic about making love in a whirlpool, but they'd never had the chance to try it. Maxwell had come along and ruined everything.

She didn't want to think about the Glencannon take-over and that part of the past, so she went to the sliding glass door and looked out at the patio. Erik had had a new section built, and she could see where the illuminated rectangular spa had been installed. The cover stood to one side, and hot water bubbled gently, sending swirls of steam into the night air.

"It's lovely," she said.

"Maybe we can try it out later. And lest you think I'm suggesting anything untoward," he added with a grin, "I do have a collection of swimsuits for guests. We won't have to go skinny-dipping—unless you want to, of course."

"We'll see," she said. "About trying it out, that is. With swimsuits," she added pointedly. "Now, can I help with anything?"

"No, it's all taken care of. But while we're waiting, would you like to have that wine out by the spa?"

She couldn't resist. "Do we have time?"

"We have all the time in the world."

Wine in hand, they went outside. It was a perfect night, warm with just the hint of a gentle breeze. A glass-topped picnic table stood to one side, and Erik held a chair for her. But instead of sitting down, she walked over and stared down at the spa.

How had this happened? she wondered. After all this time, they were seeing each other again. Only weeks ago, she never would have believed it.

She still wasn't sure she believed it. *Take it slow,* she told herself. The last thing she wanted was for history to repeat itself, especially when things were going so well.

Some of her doubts and uncertainty must have shown on her face, for Erik came up beside her and put an arm around her shoulders. He said softly, "I know what you're thinking, Rita, but I won't hurt you again. I promise."

She turned to him. "I'd like to believe that, Erik. But we didn't handle things so well before."

"I know. But that was my fault. I mean it—I want you to trust me. It's not often a person gets a second chance to make things right. Believe me, I don't want to blow it."

"I don't want to do that, either. But things seem to be moving so fast. I'm still not sure this is right."

"Maybe I'll just have to convince you all over again, then."

When he looked at her like that, how could she doubt him? And when he took her into his arms, how could she resist? Caught in a sudden wave of longing for him, she leaned against him. He held her tightly, burying his nose in her hair. As they stood there in silence, she could feel him beginning to tremble with the same passion that was rising in her. His face was half in shadow, half in wavering light from the bubbling spa when she looked up at him again, and her breath caught. She could see his eyes: they burned.

"Tell me now," he said hoarsely. "Because if I kiss you again, I won't be able to stop...."

Rita looked up at him, knowing that, no matter how she might deny it, she had been waiting for this moment. She'd been so foolish to try to ignore her attraction to him, her need...her desire. He had possessed her thoughts, he had invaded her dreams, he had remained a presence in her life even when they were apart.

And now that the moment had come, she couldn't remember why she'd had any doubts. She couldn't even recall the things they had argued about. It all seemed insignificant.

He tightened his arms around her. "Let's go inside," he whispered.

"Wait..." she murmured.

He looked surprised. "What is it?"

She shook her head. How could she explain that she wanted to stay here, in the intimate darkness with the fantasies it evoked? She was about to try, when the whirlpool began to cycle. Billows of steam rose from the surface, and the spa looked like a huge glass of champagne. When she saw that, she knew just what she wanted for this moment.

"Have you ever made love in the water?" she asked, and then smiled, putting a finger over his lips. "No, don't answer that, and neither will I. Let's just pretend it's the first time for both of us."

She didn't have to ask twice. Erik was out of his clothes in two seconds flat. He turned to help her with the buttons on her silk dress, and then with her bra and panties. She shivered slightly as he threw the flimsy garments on the chaise, and he asked in concern, "Are you cold?"

She wasn't cold, far from it. It was the sight of his nakedness that had affected her; in all her dreams and fantasies about him, she hadn't remembered just how magnificent he was.

Erik gazed at her a moment longer, then he said, "I think you're cold." Before she knew it, he swept her up into his arms and stepped with her into the tub.

The water was prickly hot, the sensation of the swirling currents erotic against Rita's bare skin. As Erik sat down on one of the seats inside the tub, still holding her, he closed his eyes. "What is it about a woman's body?" he murmured. "About *your* body...? What benevolent god made it so that it drives a man wild...?"

She had no answer, for she was wondering what clever twist of nature had designed a *man's* body so that it fit so well with a woman's. She could feel Erik's powerful thighs under her, his broad chest beneath her hands. When she looked at him again, his eyes were heavy-lidded. Sighing, he caressed her back, then began to kiss her shoulder, her throat...her lips.

Rita kissed him back, unsure whether it was the night, the warm water or Erik's gentle touch that was intoxicating her. The bubbling currents swirled around her, increasing the exotic sensations she was already feeling, and she wound her arms more tightly around him.

"Oh, Rita, what you do to me," Erik whispered. Holding her with one hand, he reached for his discarded slacks with the other and took out a small packet.

The steam made her feel flushed, and bubbles of water rose up, beading on her face and hair like sweat. The way her breasts bobbed against his chest in the water increased their sensitivity, and she gasped at the sensual awareness that rose wildly in her.

When Erik was ready, he lifted her up slightly so that he could caress her nipples with his tongue. Rita clung to him, her hips beginning to move instinctively. Positioning himself beneath her, Erik entered her with one deep thrust, and she threw her head back at the wave of ecstasy surging through her.

Water swirled and bubbled around them, between them, under and over them, pulsing against bodies already throbbing. She had never felt anything like this before: the hot water, the steam, the cool night air—and Erik moving inside her until she had to cry out her pleasure.

He uttered a hoarse sound himself, then wound his fingers in her hair and pulled her head down to his. His kiss was fierce and demanding, and he thrust his tongue into her mouth as he was thrusting himself into her very core. Their hips were moving in unison now, faster and faster as she drew him deeper inside her.

"I don't think I can..." He never finished.

As they climaxed together, their bodies rising up from the steamy water, the rush of pleasure was so powerful that Rita felt as if she were being swept up and away into the dense black sky. Dimly, she heard Erik say something, but she didn't know what. Then, gradually, she became more aware of her surroundings.

Erik had collapsed with her against the side of the spa, his eyes closed, his head back. Breathing hard herself, she leaned against him just as the timer cycled off. Slowly, the roiling water stilled, and the surface of the whirlpool became as smooth as glass.

CHAPTER TWELVE

ERIK WAS STILL IN A DAZE when he got to the office the next morning. The first thing he did when he sat down behind his desk was to call Rita. Though he had begged her not to, she had insisted on leaving his place the night before and going home. He'd wanted her to stay the night. Hell, he thought, after that extraordinary session of lovemaking in the hot tub, he wanted them to spend their entire lives together. But Rita wouldn't be swayed. She had to go home, she said; she needed time to think.

He didn't want her to think; he just wanted her to *feel*. The memory of the way her body had felt in his arms sent up a tingling ache inside him; when he thought of how the warm spa water had cascaded off her supple curves, he closed his eyes.

"Good morning. Grace DeWilde's office. How may I help you?"

It was amazing, Erik thought, how just the sound of her voice could make him want to laugh aloud. Feeling like a fatuous fool and not caring a bit, he said, "Hi."

"Hi, yourself," she said. Her voice softened. "I was hoping you'd call."

"I wanted to tell you what a wonderful time I had last night."

Huskily, she said, "Me, too."

It was that sexy tone that got to him. Trying to ignore the demanding pressure rising in his groin, he said, "You didn't have to leave last night, you know—"

"Now, Erik, we talked about that. I told you, I needed time to think."

"And have you?"

"Well, I'm still working on it."

"What is there to work on? I thought we had everything settled."

"Not everything. I don't want to rush this, Erik. I thought we agreed to take it one step at a time."

"The last thing I want to do is to pressure you. But maybe we should get together tonight and talk about it."

She laughed at that. "So soon?"

"It won't be soon enough for me. In fact, if I didn't have a full schedule today, I'd come over there right now and spirit you away."

"Oh, to where?"

"I don't know. I'd think of a place along the way. But, barring that, maybe we should talk about what we're doing tonight."

"I didn't say I could see you. How do you know I don't have plans?"

He'd never thought of that. "Do you?"

She laughed again at his dismay. Taking pity on him, she said, "As a matter of fact, I don't."

"Then what do you say?" he asked persuasively.

She thought a moment. "Well, you could come over to my house for dinner."

He laughed at the thought. "I think it would be better if I brought what we didn't get around to eating last night."

"You don't trust my cooking?"

"It's not that," he said hastily. "I just don't want you to go to any trouble."

"Oh, pizza's no trouble. The best take-out place in the world is right around the corner. Or, if you don't like that, we can always order in Chinese."

He laughed. "You've got a deal. If you like, I'll even bring it with me."

"As long as you bring yourself, I don't care."

Wondering if he could wait that long, he said, "So, what time? Would seven-thirty be all right?"

"That's fine." Seductively, she added, "And just be casual, all right? I have a feeling this won't be a formal night."

She hung up with a provocative laugh that made him feel light-headed—and in a fever for the day to be over so he could take her in his arms. On that thought, he was about to ask Eleanor to phone the florist for a huge batch of balloons to send over to her when his secretary buzzed him.

"You have a call on line one," she said. "It's Mr. Niles Madison."

Erik looked at the phone in surprise. Wondering why Caroline's father was calling him, he picked up the receiver.

"Niles? This is Erik. How are you this morning?"

His caller didn't waste time on pleasantries. "Frankly, I'm a little disturbed. I was wondering when you'd have time to discuss this matter between you and Caroline. I'd like to meet and hash it out, man to man."

Man to man? Erik thought. That irritated him almost as much as Niles's subtle emphasis on the word *when* instead of *if*. He didn't even glance at his calendar when he said, "I'm afraid my time is pretty jammed up, Niles. Can't you say whatever it is you want to say over the phone?''

"No, I can't," Niles said bluntly. "And I really think you owe me the time, Erik. After all, you and my little girl *were* discussing marriage."

He stiffened. "Who told you that?"

"Why, Caroline did, of course. You have to ask?"

"Yes, I do," Erik said sharply. "For your information, I never mentioned the word marriage to her. But even if we had talked about it, that's between Caroline and me. I'm not sure what you and I have to discuss."

"Now, now, let's not put on the gloves unless we have to," Niles said. "It's just that I'm her father, and of course I'm concerned. You know I'd do anything for Caroline. She's very unhappy that you and she have had this little disagreement, and she's asked me to talk to you about it. Surely you can take a few minutes out of your day—today, for instance—to meet me."

Erik almost said he didn't have to explain anything to Niles Madison. But Caroline's father had many powerful friends in town, and it wouldn't be smart to make an enemy of the man unless he was forced to. He had planned on canceling his noon meeting to ask Rita to lunch, but he decided he might as well get this over with right now.

"All right," he said, not bothering to disguise his irritation. "I'll meet you for lunch."

"I knew you'd see it my way," Niles said, annoying him even more. "I thought . . . my club? About twelve-thirty?"

"Fine," Erik agreed, and managed not to curse until he hung up the phone.

FOR A HUNDRED YEARS, the Spencer Club on O'Farrell Street had been for men only. Gender discrimination laws had changed that, but as Erik climbed the stone steps and entered through the heavy carved door, he reflected that, for all the women he saw, the club could still be considered a male bastion. As he walked through large rooms heavily paneled in dark woods and glanced at the windows draped in ponderous red velvets, he wondered why any woman in her right mind would want to come here.

He pictured Rita just then and smiled to himself. If she ever entered the place, the first thing she'd do would be to pull the thick draperies aside and throw open the windows to let in some fresh air. Even though he enjoyed a cigar himself on occasion, the odor of stale smoke made his nostrils contract, and he went quickly to the main dining room.

Niles was already waiting for him, at a table near an oil painting of a hunting dog holding a dead bird in its mouth. Erik had always wondered why decorators put pictures like that in dining rooms, but since the place was full of them, he averted his eyes and tried to gauge the other man's mood.

Niles Madison was in his seventies, but with his full head of silvery white hair, he looked a good ten years younger. He tried to keep his weight down with workouts here in the exercise room of the club, but he was still portly, with a round, florid face and wire-framed bifocal glasses. He looked up at Erik's approach and smiled broadly.

Erik immediately mistrusted that smile. As he took the chair opposite, he said warily, "Hello, Niles."

"Hello, Erik. Thanks for coming. I know how busy you are."

"No problem," Erik said politely. "Now, what's this about?"

Niles sat back. At a gesture from him, a dark-suited waiter came forward bearing a tray with two highball glasses. Without a word, the man set the glasses on the table and disappeared.

"I took the liberty of ordering drinks," Niles said. "Are Manhattans all right?"

Erik loathed Manhattans, but he nodded. He even picked up the glass and took a sip when Niles saluted with his. Then he put the drink down and said, "I really don't have much time—"

"I appreciate that, Erik, so I'll get right to the point. As I told you, Caroline is most distressed about this little misunderstanding you and she have had, and I'd like to do what I can to help put things right."

Erik had already decided that the only way to handle this was to be direct. "I'm afraid that isn't possible. There was no misunderstanding. I told Caroline that I couldn't see her anymore. It's as simple as that."

The older man's pale blue eyes glinted behind the glasses. "Oh, I don't think so, Erik. You see, my little girl has her heart set on marrying you."

Erik's jaw tightened. *And what Caroline wants, Caroline gets, was that it?* "I'm sorry if Caroline—"

Niles sat forward. Deliberately misconstruing what Erik had started to say, he said, "I know you're sorry. That's why I wanted to meet and talk. I'm sure we can figure out how to rectify this situation."

"There is no situation, Niles. In fact—"

"I'm not sure you understand," Niles interrupted heavily. His eyes rested unwaveringly on Erik's face as he emphasized, "I do want to work this out."

As irked as he was about the man's interference in something that was, after all, none of his business, Erik was still determined to handle the situation without losing his cool. "I appreciate your concern," he began carefully, "but there's nothing anyone can do. The fact is—and I told Caroline this—our relationship just didn't work."

"But have you really given it a chance?"

Erik was about to reply when he reminded himself that Caroline was an only child whose parents were slavishly devoted to her. Naturally, they didn't want to see her hurt. He hadn't wanted to hurt her, either. He respected everyone's feelings, but he still couldn't change his own—not to suit Caroline, or to please Niles and Pamela Madison.

"You're a man of the world, Niles. You know that sometimes things just happen. I thought I loved Caroline. I really did want to make the relationship work. But when I realized it wasn't meant to be, I did the honorable thing and told her so."

"But Caroline wasn't the only one who thought you and she were the perfect couple," Niles said, as though that made everything right. "Pamela and I always thought so, too. We were eager to accept you into our family. In fact, her mother and I were looking forward to giving you both a big wedding with all the trimmings."

"That's a nice idea, but—"

"Our gift to you was to be your honeymoon—wherever in the world you wanted it to be—and then we planned to welcome you into our home."

Despite his vow not to lose his temper, Erik could feel his control beginning to fray at the seams. "You seem to have had everything planned."

Niles waved a hand. Now came the man-to-man part, Erik thought. "It wasn't me," Niles said. "You know how women are. I really believe they start to design a daughter's wedding the day the little girls are born."

"If that's true, I'm sorry to have to disappoint Pamela. And you, too. But I can't marry your daughter, Niles."

Niles didn't reply for a long moment. Then he said meaningfully, "I'm sure we can figure out a way to change your position."

"And I'm sure we can't. Now, if you don't mind—"

Deciding the conversation was over, he started to get up, but Niles reached across the table and grasped his arm. Startled and annoyed by the gesture, Erik looked from Niles's hand to his face.

"Please, sit down, Erik," Niles said calmly, "I thought you might end the discussion this way, so I came prepared. I have a proposition for you."

Erik didn't want to wrestle the older man. Nor did he want to hear whatever else Niles had to say. But short of wrenching his arm free, he didn't seem to have any other choice. His jaw clenched, he sat down again.

"Thank you," Niles said. "Now, I think part of the problem, Erik, is that you've been working too hard."

Erik wasn't going to listen to a lecture about his work habits—especially not from a man who had, by his own admission, spent almost every waking minute in his own office before he semiretired. Even now, Niles went to the office almost every day, if only to look at the mail.

"I like working hard, Niles. It's what I do."

"I understand that. In fact, I'm exactly the same. Now that I'm retired, of course, things are different. But even when I was younger—like you—and the pressure for more and better accounts was tremendous, I enjoyed the challenge. In fact, I reveled in it. There were times when I felt that even if I worked twenty-six hours a day, it wouldn't be enough."

Erik felt the same way. But he asked, "And your point is?"

"My point is that it took me until my retirement to realize that when we get locked into such a frantic pace, other things—more important things—fall by the wayside. We're just too busy to care or to take the time to change our lives."

"I don't want to change my life. I like it just the way it is."

"So you believe now. But what I'm trying to tell you is that sometimes we don't realize what a toll our work habits take on ourselves and our loved ones. I don't want you to look back with regret when it's too late. I want to help you now."

"I don't want any help. I told you, I enjoy my work."

"So did I. But I could make your work even more enjoyable, Erik. It's been quite a while since we discussed that vice presidency I offered you. Perhaps we should talk about it now."

Insulted by the flagrant attempt at bribery, Erik replied, "I don't think so. As I told you before when you mentioned it, I'm perfectly happy with my own firm."

"It wouldn't be impossible for you to manage both."

"I think it would be."

"I wouldn't be so hasty if I were you."

"I'm not being hasty. We've already discussed this—"

"We haven't discussed the Sutcliff project."

There it was. Erik knew they had come to the real purpose of this meeting, and he felt a corresponding tightening in his gut. Sutcliff was the international hotel project that Phil Soames was involved in—or that Phil wanted to be involved in. But it was also an undertaking that Erik had put out of his mind long ago.

Or thought he had.

"What about it?" he said.

Satisfied that he had Erik's attention, Niles sat back, toying with his glass. "It seems to be quite a project. In fact, it will undoubtedly be a plum for anyone who's in on the ground floor. Don't you think so?"

Erik shrugged. "If it's a success, it wouldn't hurt a résumé."

Niles smiled. It wasn't a particularly pleasant smile. "How would you like to be involved?"

"I don't have time."

Niles looked at him in disbelief. "Not even for something on that scale?"

"Not even then," Erik insisted. "I've got too much to do right now."

"Well, that's a shame."

"Why?"

"Because I know Bob Sutcliff very well. In fact, we go back a long way. We're old fraternity brothers. And on occasion, we've done favors for each other."

"What does that have to do with me?"

"If you were . . . say, part of the family, I could put a good word in for you with Bob. He usually listens to me."

But Erik was no longer listening to Niles. Tantalizing images of revenge on Phil Soames flashed through his mind, and suddenly he knew that he'd give just about anything to take the Sutcliff project away from the man who had once been his best friend. Ever since the Glencannon affair, he'd been itching to pay Phil back for the fast one he'd pulled. The thought that the means might be at hand made him salivate; the fact that Phil already had a lot of his own money invested in acquiring the project made the idea of such a coup even sweeter.

Then reality returned. He could do all this, he thought, but at what price?

Niles had been watching him closely. As their eyes met, he said softly, "We're both men of the world, Erik. I want you to know I'd do anything for my son-in-law." He paused. "Anything."

"That obviously includes trying to bribe someone to marry your daughter."

The eyes behind the wire-framed glasses turned cold. "You shouldn't take such a narrow view of things, Erik. Especially when a refusal on your part could have...untoward consequences."

"Are you threatening me?"

"That's rather melodramatic, don't you think? Let's just say that it's better to count me as a friend than an enemy."

Erik was so furious he could hardly speak. What he wanted to do was to throttle the man. He made himself stand. "In that case," he said, "I'll avoid both. Forgive me if I don't stay for lunch."

RITA HADN'T HAD such a good day in longer than she could remember. She'd talked to Erik that morning, and tonight they were going to have dinner together. *And whatever else might transpire,* she thought wickedly, and wanted to laugh aloud with sheer joy. Wasn't life grand?

Then Erik called again, just as she was about to go home, and burst her bubble.

"Hi," he said when she rushed back to catch the phone. "I've got bad news."

She knew at once. "You can't come tonight, right?"

"No, I can't," he said. "Something came up, and I have to catch a flight to Chicago in about an hour. In fact, I'm calling from the car because I'm on my way to the airport right now."

She tried to hide her disappointment. "But what happened?"

"Some clients have an emergency that they insist only I can resolve—in person. I'll make it as quick a trip as I can. Please try to understand."

"Oh . . . I do," she said. And she did. But that didn't mean she had to be happy about it. "When do you think you'll get back?"

"It shouldn't take but a couple of days, at most. Oh, Rita, I did want to see you tonight. . . ."

"I wanted to see you, too."

"We'll make up for it when I get back."

She tried to smile. "I'll hold you to that."

"Goodbye, love. Take care."

"You, too," she said forlornly. She hung up, but the phone rang almost instantly again. Hoping it was Erik calling back, she snatched up the receiver. "Yes?"

A voice she didn't recognize said, "I'd like to speak to Miss Rita Shannon, please."

"This is she."

"My name is Pamela Madison. I'd like to talk to you about something if I might. Would that be possible, say, tonight?"

Rita knew who Pamela Madison was; who in this town didn't? The woman was always showing up in the society pages. She was known for participating in all sorts of causes, and she attended numerous fund-raisers. But what could Pamela Madison want with her?

"Could you tell me what it's about?" she asked.

"I'd rather discuss that when we meet."

"Are you sure you have the right person?" Rita asked. Grace had already left for an appointment, but she added, "If you wish to talk to Mrs. DeWilde—"

"No, I want to talk to you. Will you come?"

"Well, I was just leaving work—"

"Perfect. Would the lounge at the Pan Pacific be convenient? It's not too far from your office."

Rita frowned. How did Pamela Madison know where she worked? For that matter, how had the woman gotten hold of this number? It occurred to her that this might be something to do with Grace—a surprise, perhaps? Curious now, she said, "All right. I can be there in a few minutes."

"Excellent. I'll be waiting for you."

As promised, Pamela Madison was sitting by herself at a table for two in the lounge of the new hotel when Rita came in. Rita recognized her at once from her newspaper pictures. She was wearing a gray suit with matching heels, and not a light brown hair was out of place. She reminded Rita of Grace, except that, even from across the room, it was obvious she lacked Grace's warmth. Her eyes were cool as Rita approached, and without a word, she gestured to the other chair.

"Thank you for coming, Miss Shannon," she said. "Would you like a drink?"

"Nothing, thank you." From the way the woman was looking at her, Rita suspected that she wouldn't be here long enough to finish it.

"Fine. I'll get right to the point, then. You've been seeing Erik Mulholland, haven't you?"

Rita knew then that this wasn't about a surprise for Grace. Erik hadn't told her what Caroline's surname was, but it was obvious now. Her own voice cool, she replied, "Yes, I have been seeing him. Is that what this is about?"

"As a matter of fact, yes. Now, I'd rather not make this unpleasant for either of us, but you should know at the outset that I love my daughter very much. So does her father. What makes her unhappy makes us unhappy, and she's extremely upset about this...situation with Erik."

Already, Rita didn't like where this was going. "Oh," she said. "And what situation is that?"

Pamela looked at her in well-bred surprise. "You seem like an intelligent girl. Surely I don't have to spell it out for you."

No, you surely don't, Rita thought, beginning to get angry. Just who did this woman think she was? And even more to the point, what was wrong with Caroline? If she wanted Erik back, why didn't she come herself to say it? Why send her mother?

"I'm afraid you do have to spell it out." She didn't care if Pamela Madison was Queen of San Francisco; she was not going to be pushed around. "Because, frankly, I don't have the faintest idea what you're talking about."

A flash of irritation crossed Pamela Madison's smooth face. "I see," she said. "You're going to be difficult about this."

"It depends on what you mean by difficult," Rita said. "If you mean, am I going to continue seeing Erik, yes, I am. Is he going to continue seeing me? Yes again. And, not that it's any of your business, I really don't see how you can stop either of us."

"I don't think you understand. My husband and I have a great deal of influence in this city—in the entire state, in fact. We can make things extremely unpleasant for you—"

Rita looked at her incredulously. "Are you threatening me?"

"I don't threaten. It's not necessary."

Rita's temper was shredding by the second. Rashly, she said, "Well, fine, go ahead and give it your best shot. You don't intimidate me. And while I can't speak for Erik, I know you won't intimidate him, either. Now, I'm sorry Caroline is upset, but she's just going to have to be a big girl and accept the fact that their relationship is over."

"You're wrong," Pamela Madison said. Her light gray eyes were as cold as the Bering Strait. "Because, you see, my husband met with Erik today and made him an offer he couldn't refuse." She paused. "An offer he *won't* refuse."

Fiercely, Rita willed her expression not to change. But even as she sat there, her mind instantly flashed to Erik's sudden business trip. She hadn't thought much about it at the time, but now she wondered—and hated herself for it—just why he'd had to leave in such a hurry.

She glanced covertly at the other woman. Was Pamela Madison telling the truth, or was she just making up a story to cast doubt and suspicion? Well, if it was the latter, she thought agitatedly, she'd done a good job. Now Erik's abrupt departure had taken on a sinister meaning.

"Is that so," she managed to say. "And what offer was that?"

"I don't think we need to go into it. Suffice it to say, it was something that will give Erik everything he's ever wanted."

"And all he has to do is to drop me and start seeing Caroline again?"

Pamela Madison looked at her pityingly. "Oh, my dear, you really don't get it, do you. Erik isn't going to *date* Caroline. He's going to marry her."

"I don't believe you," Rita said flatly, while inside her heart was beginning to pound like a jackhammer. "He wouldn't do that. Or, at least, he wouldn't do that without telling me."

"Are you certain of that?"

"Yes, I am," Rita said, although at the moment she was less and less certain. Why *had* Erik taken off so abruptly? What was in Chicago that she didn't know about?

"Then perhaps you'd better ask him," Pamela Madison said. She raised a finger. "No, wait, you can't do that, can you. Hasn't he gone off on a sudden business trip to Chicago?"

How had she known that? Rita wondered. Unwillingly, she had to admit that it gave credence to what she'd said. But even so, she thought, she was not going to let Pamela Madison see how rattled she was. And since the woman already knew about Erik's trip, she saw no reason to deny it. "As a matter of fact, Erik *has* gone away on business."

"Do you know why?"

"Certainly I do. A client of his had an emergency."

"That's what he told you?"

"That's what happened!" Rita said sharply. For good measure, she added, "And it didn't have anything to do with your husband or your daughter."

Pamela Madison smiled. It wasn't a pleasant sight. "You're sure of that."

"Yes, I am." She had heard enough. Heatedly, she sat forward. "Look, Mrs. Madison—"

"Since you're so sure, perhaps you'd better call a man named Phil Soames and find out what he has to say about it."

Rita sat back. "I don't know anyone named Phil Soames."

"Oh, but Erik does. And I suggest that you call him. He'll be able to confirm what I've been telling you about what my husband can do for Erik." A superior look on her face, she reached for her purse, opened it and took out a card, which she placed on the table between them. "I suspected you might not believe me, so I took the liberty of obtaining Mr. Soames's Los Angeles phone number."

Rita forced herself not to even glance at the card. "And why," she asked, "would I call Mr. Soames, when I can just talk to Erik?"

"Because," Pamela Madison said patronizingly, "Erik is going to be out of touch for a few days. And when he finally does get back, the deal will be done."

"I don't believe you," Rita retorted, but despite herself, her voice shook.

"Believe what you like. But don't say I didn't warn you."

"Erik would never take a bribe!"

The woman gave her another pitying look. "Oh, it wasn't a *bribe,* Miss Shannon. In one sense, it was business as usual—but on a more personal level. My daughter will get what she wants, and so will Erik. And there's not a thing you can do about it."

"We'll see about that!"

Pamela Madison stood. "Call Mr. Soames, dear, and save yourself a great deal of embarrassment."

CHAPTER THIRTEEN

IT WAS AFTER DINNERTIME when Rita finally got home, but she was so agitated that she couldn't eat. She wanted a glass of wine, but with her stomach in knots, she settled for a cup of tea and took it out onto the deck. She needed to think.

"It was lies, all lies," she told herself shakily. She willed herself to believe that if Erik had said he was going on an emergency business trip to help a client, that's exactly what he had done. But Pamela Madison had been so sure of herself that, despite her faith in Erik, she had doubts. Maybe he *had* created such an elaborate ruse because he'd accepted a bribe to marry Caroline Madison. Maybe—

She put the tea down with a clatter. She couldn't accept it. She wouldn't.

But before she could stop it, suspicion rose again like a poison mushroom in a black cave of her mind. Maybe Erik hadn't gone to Chicago, she thought. Maybe he was still here in the city. Maybe he and Caroline had gone to Reno, or Monaco. How would she know?

"You know!" she said aloud. "You know he wouldn't do that. Not after what happened before. He just wouldn't!"

She had to get a grip on herself. She was getting worked up, and with what proof? Could she really believe a woman who had admitted that she'd do anything for her daughter? It was obvious that Pamela Madison had meant every word she'd said; if she wanted a marriage to take place between Caroline and Erik, it seemed equally clear that she would say anything to hurry the process along.

You see, my husband met with Erik today and made him an offer he couldn't refuse. An offer he won't refuse.

As Pamela's words whipped through her mind, Rita sank deeper into the deck chair. Perhaps, for the sake of argument, she could assume—for a few minutes, anyway—that what she had said was true. Rita still couldn't imagine what offer Pamela Madison was talking about. It couldn't be mere money; Erik could make that on his own. It had to be something else, something big, or Erik wouldn't give it a second thought. He was already a major success with Mulholland-Laughton; what more could he want?

What was she thinking? She, of all people, knew how ambitious Erik was; if she had any doubts, all she had to do was to remember the Glencannon takeover last year. He'd been like a shark.

She didn't want to think about Glencannon's, which she had tried to put to rest. But she knew that whatever the Madisons had offered Erik, it had to be on that scale at least. What could it be?

She frowned, trying to remember what she had read about the Madisons in the paper. All she could recall was that Niles Madison was a partner in a big San Francisco investment firm—

She bolted upright. That was it! Niles Madison had offered Erik a partnership!

She slumped again. No, she was way off base. Why would Erik shut down his own company to work with

Niles Madison? And what about Rudy? It had to be something else.

She was going in circles, getting more confused and upset with each go-around. Her head had started to pound; she couldn't think straight. In fact, she didn't *want* to think about it anymore. What she really wanted was for Erik to come home so she could ask him directly if Pamela Madison had been telling the truth.

She rubbed her temple, wishing she'd had the foresight to ask where he was staying in Chicago. If she knew that, she could stop all these wild speculations by calling his hotel. In fact, the way she felt right now, she probably would have taken a plane out tonight herself. More than anything, she wanted to get this straightened out.

Erik is going to be out of touch for a few days. And when he finally does get back, the deal will be done....

When Pamela's voice flashed into her mind once more, she winced. What *deal?* And why would Erik be out of touch? Nothing about this made any sense.

The tea hadn't helped her stomach; she felt as if she were going to be sick. She had to calm down. Otherwise, she'd go off the deep end and be a wreck long before Erik came home. *If* he did.

"He's coming home," she muttered to herself. "Don't be more ridiculous than you've already been."

She had to do something; she couldn't just sit here and speculate. Maybe she should just have some warm milk and go to bed. Weren't things supposed to look better in the morning?

Wearily, she stood. But as she went into the house, an idea suddenly occurred to her. She could check out one part of the story, she thought. Tomorrow morning, first thing, she'd call Rudy Laughton and ask if he knew how to contact Erik. If anyone knew where Erik was, it would be his partner. And once she had the information, she'd call the hotel and tell Erik...

What?

The truth, she decided. She'd tell him the truth. She'd repeat what Pamela Madison had had to say tonight, and then she'd ask him what he thought. One thing she knew: this time, she wasn't going to judge Erik—not until she heard his side of the story. If she doubted him every time something came up, they'd never be able to work out any kind of meaningful relationship.

She felt better after she'd made that decision, and she washed out her cup and put it in the dish rack to dry. She'd thrown her purse and briefcase on the counter when she first came home, and she was picking them up when she remembered the card Pamela Madison had given her. She'd put it in her purse.

Slowly, she unzipped the flap. She took the card out and stared at it. Was Phil Soames one of Pamela Madison's red herrings, or did he really know something about this?

She glanced at the clock. It was just after nine. Maybe she should call Mr. Soames and—

Quickly, she stuffed the card back into her purse. She wasn't going to call anyone—at least, not tonight. She'd already decided that she'd wait until she heard what Erik's partner had to say, and that's what she'd do. Resolutely, she left the purse and briefcase where they were and switched off the kitchen light. She rarely retired before eleven, but tonight was going to be an exception. She was exhausted; all she wanted to do was climb into bed, pull the covers over her head and deal with this in the morning.

DESPITE HER EARLY NIGHT, Rita was late for work. She still felt groggy and out of sorts when she arrived, but it seemed her troubles on this new day were just beginning. Grace was already at her desk, and as soon as she saw her employer's face, she knew something was wrong.

"I just took the oddest call," Grace said. "It was Ben, our contractor."

Because she'd never seen Grace look so shocked, Rita had thought the problem involved someone in Grace's family. Relieved that this was probably something they could easily handle, she asked, "What did he want?"

"He said that the bank denied him access to the construction funds account."

She'd started toward her own desk, but at Grace's words, she stopped. "*What?* Why?"

"Because of insufficient funds."

"But that's impossible. I went over the bank statements just the other day when Ben told me he was about to put in a big construction order. There was plenty of money. It has to be a mistake."

"That's what I thought. So I called the bank."

"And?"

"And they said that the automatic transfer of funds into that account had not . . . occurred."

Rita felt a stab of uneasiness. Last night, Pamela Madison had said that she could make things very unpleasant unless Rita was a good little girl and stood back so that Miss Caroline could have her way. Was this a hint of what the Madisons could do?

She was being absurd again. It had to be a coincidence. Instead of imagining things, she should focus on the business at hand. "I don't understand. We've never had any trouble before."

"That's what makes it so strange," Grace said. "I requested that the bank check their records regarding all transactions to that account, and they agreed to do it as soon as possible."

"Today, I hope?"

"This morning. They're going to call us back. In the meantime, I tried to call Erik, but Eleanor said he had to make an emergency trip to Chicago. Did you know about that?"

"Yes, he called me from the car on the way to the airport. It was right after you'd left last night." Rita had decided not to mention her meeting with Pamela Madison until she had talked to Erik.

Obviously frustrated, Grace said, "I guess there's nothing we can do except wait."

Rita felt too unsettled to sit around until the phone rang. "I knew we shouldn't have agreed to four separate payments," she muttered.

"The terms were reasonable at the time," Grace pointed out. "And because Erik was able to get the investors to agree that I wouldn't have to pay full interest until the money was in my account, I didn't want to haggle. As we're all painfully aware, the investment potential for retail stores right now is tight enough. If his people were willing to put up the money, I didn't care how many payments there were, just as long as the funds were there when we needed them."

"Well, that was fine as long as everything worked according to plan," Rita said, and thought of something. "Uh-oh."

"I'm sure I don't like the sound of that. What is it now?"

Her face glum, Rita went to her desk and took out a folder. Inside was a huge inventory list for the store.

Gingerly holding it up with her fingertips so that Grace could see it, she said, "I called this in yesterday before I left."

Grace knew at a glance what it was; they'd been working on it for weeks now. Her own face falling, she sat back in her chair. "Well, as they say, this is a fine mess. If the bank isn't releasing nonexistent funds to the contractor, they're certainly not going to pay for that order."

"Do you want me to call the companies involved and cancel?" Rita asked. "Or I could ask them to put the order on hold."

"And what excuse could we give?" Grace asked. "I don't think we should say there's been a tiny little slip-up where our funds are concerned."

"I think I'll go down to the bank," Rita said. "Maybe if I'm there, we can get this straightened out sooner."

"Good idea. In the meantime, I'll make a few calls of my own. It could be that this problem has originated . . . elsewhere."

Rita was already on her way out. "Elsewhere? What do you mean?"

"At first I thought of Jeffrey," Grace said unwillingly. "But even though he hasn't been pleased by my new endeavor, I doubt he'd do something like this. However, there are others I could name who might want to throw a wrench in my plans."

"Oh, I hope not," Rita said.

"So do I," Grace agreed grimly. "But we should cover all avenues."

RITA THOUGHT ABOUT Grace's remark on her way back from an unsatisfactory visit to the bank. She'd gone through reams of paperwork there; she and the person assigned to help her had checked every figure and amount. But the money that should have been deposited to cover Grace's expenses hadn't been transferred into the account. And no one knew why.

"But it *has* to be here!" Rita exclaimed after they'd gone over it for the fourth time.

"I'm sorry, Ms. Shannon," the equally frustrated bank officer told her. "I don't know what happened."

"Money doesn't just disappear," she insisted. "It has to be somewhere."

"As you know, we do transfer funds electronically. The only way I can think for this to have occurred is that someone who knew how to do it accessed the account."

"Then find out who it was," she demanded.

"We're working on it, I assure you. We want to get to the bottom of this just as much as you do."

Rita doubted that, but there wasn't much more she could do. She left the bank wishing she didn't have to go back and tell Grace that they just had to wait. As she was passing Erik's office building, she saw a parking space. Before she could think about it, she pulled in. Why call Rudy when she could talk to him in person?

Eleanor was at her desk when Rita entered Erik's office. "Why, good afternoon, Ms. Shannon," the secretary greeted her. "I'm sorry, but Erik isn't here."

"I know," Rita said. "I didn't come to see him. I realize I should have called for an appointment, but I'd like to speak to Rudy if I may. It won't take long."

"Did I hear my name?" Rudy asked. He'd come in behind her, and when she turned, he gave her a smile.

"Hello, Rudy," she said. "Do you have a few minutes?"

"Always. Come on in."

She went with him to his office down the hall. He gestured her to a chair, then took one himself. "What can I do for you?"

Now that she was here, she didn't know where to begin. In fact, she wasn't really sure why she had come. Erik and Rudy were partners; if something was going on, wouldn't Rudy cover for Erik?

Ashamed of the thought, she said quickly, "I'm sorry to bother you, Rudy, but with Erik gone—"

"Yes, he had to go to Chicago last night after an emergency call from one of our clients. He's supposed to be away only a day or two, but with Gelberg Industries, one never knows."

Rita had never heard of Gelberg Industries, and just for an instant, she wondered—

What does it matter? she asked herself impatiently. She had to get control of these wild suspicions. After all, just because she wasn't familiar with the company didn't mean it didn't exist.

"Is something wrong?" Rudy asked.

"Wrong?" she repeated, stalling for time. What was she going to tell him? Then she looked into his kind, open face and thought that if she had to trust someone, it might as well be him. She took a deep breath. "I need to talk to Erik," she said. "Could you tell me what hotel he's staying at?"

"Oh, I'm sorry, he's not staying at a hotel." Rudy grimaced. "In fact, that's why Erik went instead of me. I'm allergic to nature, but Erik can put up with Mr. Outdoors, as we call Herbert Gelberg. Whenever there's a meeting, Gelberg insists that it take place at his lodge, miles from anywhere."

"But surely the place has a telephone!"

He shook his head. "Not even a television. The man is a real eccentric. He won't even allow cellulars to be brought in." He rolled his eyes. "Such modern conveniences would mar the unspoiled beauty of the place, he says. If you ask me, the guy's a complete crackpot."

Rita looked at him in dismay. She hadn't anticipated this. "So there's no way to get in touch with him?"

"Not unless it's a real emergency. Then, I suppose we could call the sheriff or the highway patrol or Search and Rescue." Rudy paused. "*Is* there an emergency?"

"Well, I'm not sure. We're having a problem with the bank this morning. They say there are no funds in the store account."

"That's impossible. I know Erik authorized another payment before he left."

Rita felt another stab of dread, which she suppressed by sheer will. Just because Erik had authorized a payment that had never shown up didn't mean that he had diverted the money elsewhere, did it? But she was still painfully aware that if anyone could fudge an electronic transfer, it would be Erik. He knew all about that kind of thing.

She had to stop this, she told herself. "There's been a mix-up, then, because the money isn't there," she told Rudy.

He immediately reached for the phone. "I'll call the bank myself. Don't worry, we'll get this straightened out."

"Wait—"

He turned back to her, phone in hand. "There's something else?"

She hadn't intended to ask, but the words were out before she could stop them. "Rudy," she said, "have you ever heard of a man named Phil Soames?"

Slowly, Rudy put down the phone. "Where did you hear about him?"

She didn't want to say. "Oh, his name came up the other day," she said vaguely. "Do you know him?"

He appeared to be thinking carefully before he answered. Finally, he said, "Yes, I know him."

Ignoring his obvious reluctance to talk about the man, she leaned forward. "What can you tell me about him?"

He seemed to be debating what to say again. "Well, he owns a Los Angeles-based investment firm—like this one."

"And? Go on."

He got up. Avoiding her eyes, he said, "There's really nothing to go on with. He's just... another businessman."

She stared at him. Then she said quietly, "Why are you lying to me?"

"I'm not lying," he started to say, but after a glance at her face, he sat down again and sighed. "Look, I think it would be better if you discussed this with Erik."

"I'd like to discuss it with him. But he's out of touch for a few days, remember? So, I'm asking you. Is there anything I should know about this Phil Soames?"

"I really can't tell you that, Rita. As I said, Erik is the one who's had a problem with Phil."

"What kind of problem?"

Rudy sighed again. "It's up to him to tell you—if he wants to."

She was getting angry. "And if he doesn't want to?"

Rudy was silent.

"I see," she said, and stood. Unable to keep the bitterness out of her voice, she added, "Thanks for nothing, Rudy."

He rose, too, as unhappy as she was. "I'm sorry, Rita. But I really do feel that this is Erik's business. You'll understand when you talk to him."

"Yes, sure. And in the meantime, I guess we all just wait for the big man to come home again, right?"

He winced. "I'll have him call you the instant he gets in."

She almost told him not to bother, but she wasn't going to let her temper get the best of her—not this time. She *was* going to talk to Erik, and they *were* going to get this straightened out. But as she left the office and went out to her car, she decided that while she was waiting, maybe a quick phone call to Los Angeles wouldn't hurt.

GRACE WAS SITTING on the living room couch when Rita got back to the office. She sat up quickly. "Any news?"

"Nothing that we didn't already know," Rita said, throwing her stuff down on her desk. "The bank is still working on it."

Grace sighed. "I'm afraid that I wasn't any more successful than you. Nothing came of those calls I made to DeWilde headquarters. In fact, everyone was terribly surprised that I had the gall to accuse them. I do believe they weren't involved."

"I stopped in to see Rudy on the way back here, and he's promised to give the bank a little push. But in the meantime, I think I'll just start calling Erik's investors. Someone has to know something about this."

"But I thought this business with the account was just a mistake."

Oh, it was a mistake, all right, Rita thought. But exactly what kind, she wasn't sure yet. The problem with the bank, combined with Erik's quick trip to Chicago, his being incommunicado and Rudy's obvious evasiveness, seemed to point to one thing: someone was up to no good. And when she thought back to the Glencannon takeover last year, she was pretty sure she knew who that someone was.

She reached for the phone. "We're going to find out," she said.

She found out, all right. Erik had been cagey about providing the names of his investors—to protect everyone's interests, he'd said. But Rita hadn't let that deter her. While at the bank this morning, she'd managed to get a glimpse of some interesting paperwork concerning Grace's account. She hadn't wanted to be so obvious as to write down telephone numbers, but names would serve her purpose just as well. And fortunately, she thought, she had a memory for names. She remembered every one.

For the next few hours, she called each person on the list she'd made when she left the bank. She explained what had happened, and she asked if they had changed their minds about backing Grace. The replies were framed differently, but the content was the same: No one could help her. She'd have to ask Erik.

When she said goodbye to the last person, she was so upset she could hardly speak. She was almost ready to hire a wilderness guide to take her to the lodge where Erik was supposedly staying and confront him directly. Instead, her final call was to Rudy. Without preamble, she asked him if he'd gotten the problem with Grace's account straightened out.

"No," he said, sounding strange. "But I'm still working on it."

It was as she had expected: Rudy was in on it, too, or else he was covering, as a good partner would, for Erik.

"Thanks," she said coldly. "Will you call us when you have some news?"

He promised to do so, but she didn't believe him anymore. It was almost six o'clock when she hung up the phone, time to go home.

"Are you sure you're going to be all right, Grace?" she asked anxiously as she gathered her things.

"I'll be fine," Grace said wearily. "As my grandmother said, things always look better in the morning."

That axiom certainly hadn't held true for today, Rita couldn't help thinking, but she didn't say anything. Trying to be optimistic when she felt anything but, she said, "We'll get it settled on Monday."

"I know we will."

Rita thought about the situation all the way home. She couldn't remember the last time she'd had such a frustrating, unproductive day, and all she wanted to do was to forget the whole thing. But over and over again she remembered what all those people had told her this afternoon: Ask Erik. He'd be able to tell her if anything had gone wrong.

Her face grim, she parked the car in her driveway. *Ask Erik*, she thought contemptuously. Well, she'd do that in good time. But right now, she was going to phone someone else. It was time, she thought as she unlocked her front door and slammed it behind her, to talk to Phil Soames.

CHAPTER FOURTEEN

RITA WAS JUST HEADING for the phone when it rang. At this point, she was so on edge that she jumped violently at the sound and just stared at it for a few seconds. Then it rang again, and as if it were a snake that might bite her, she reached for the receiver. After all this time of wanting to speak to Erik, she didn't know what she'd say if he was calling. Cursing herself for not allowing the answering machine to screen the call for her, she said a cautious hello.

"Hi, Reetz," Marie said cheerfully. "I'm so glad you're home. I'm calling to ask you and Erik to dinner next weekend. Can you make it? Friday or Saturday night—either one is fine with me. You choose."

Rita's racing heart settled back into a steady rhythm—until she realized she didn't know what to say to her sister. If she refused the invitation outright, Marie would want to know why. But she could hardly say that she didn't think she and Erik would be able to come because by then they might not be speaking to each other.

"Next weekend isn't a good time," she said. "Could we take a rain check?"

She never had been able to hide anything from Marie, who immediately asked, "What's wrong?"

"Nothing's wrong," she lied. "I'm just tired. It's been a long day."

Marie was silent a beat. "I get it. You don't want to talk about it, right?"

"There's nothing to talk about. I told you—"

"Oh, Reetz," Marie said with a sigh, "you scared him off, didn't you?"

"I didn't *scare* him off," Rita said, although when she thought about it, it didn't seem like a bad idea. Hastily she added, "It's just that Erik had to go out of town on a business trip, and I don't know when he'll be back."

"Are you sure that's all?"

"Positive."

"Well, then," Marie said, sounding relieved. "You know how casual things are here. I don't need to know right now. In fact, you can call me as late as Friday, if you like."

"Okay, fine. I'll let you know," Rita said, trying to disguise her anxiety. She wanted to get off the phone and call the Soames number before she lost courage.

"Are you in a hurry?" Marie asked. "Is this a bad time?"

"I just have to make a couple of business calls," Rita told her, staring at the card she was still holding. She was so tense that she'd crumpled it into a little ball. "How about if I call you tomorrow?"

"Well, all right. But—" Marie hesitated. "Are you sure everything's okay with you?"

Rita thought that things couldn't be worse. But she didn't want to get into it with Marie, so she said, "Everything's fine. Grace and I just had a problem with the bank today. It's still not straightened out, and now we have to wait until Monday."

"I see. I understand how frustrating that can be. But you sound strange, Reetz."

"I told you, I'm just tired. After I get through with these calls, I'm going to fall into bed and sleep until noon tomorrow. Then I'll be okay."

"Lucky you," Marie said enviously. "All right, then, I guess I'll say good-night. But do try to come next weekend. I wasn't supposed to tell you, but Betsy has a surprise planned for Erik. She's been working on it ever since he took you both to see the *Phantom.*"

"A surprise?" Rita said faintly.

"Yes, you know how much she loved the show. Well, she's fixed up a stage, and she's been practicing a play she wrote to show where the Phantom goes to heal his broken heart. It's really quite clever, if I do say so myself. She'll be so disappointed if you two can't come."

"We'll try to make it," Rita said. But she had to add, "But don't promise her, okay? I really don't know what's going to happen by next weekend."

She hung up before Marie could ask what she'd meant. Biting her lip, she smoothed out the card with Soames's number on it. She glanced at the clock. It was almost eight; would he still be at work? It was now or never, she thought. She took a deep breath and dialed Los Angeles.

The phone rang three times at the other end before it was picked up. "Soames," a male voice said.

She'd been half hoping that he wouldn't be in, or that he wouldn't answer his own phone. But now that she had him on the line, she had to say, "Mr. Soames, my name is Rita Shannon. I'm calling to—"

"Rita Shannon," he repeated. "I know that name. Just a minute—wait, I've got it. You were going out with Erik during that Glencannon business last year, right?"

Rita was nonplussed. How had he known that? She knew she had never met Phil Soames, but there was no point in denying the truth of what he'd said, so she replied, "As a matter of fact, I was."

"I thought so. I never forget a name."

"That's . . . admirable, Mr. Soames. Now, if I might get to the reason I'm calling?"

"Sure, go ahead."

"I'm afraid this is a little awkward, but a woman named Pamela Madison gave me your name. She told me—"

Just like that, he dropped the polite tone. "I can imagine what *she* said. So, are you calling to commiserate or to gloat?"

A chill ran down Rita's spine. The fact that he could ask such a question wasn't a good sign. Cautiously, she said, "I'm not sure what you mean."

"You want me to spell it out? Well, fine. We've both been screwed by Erik Mulholland, haven't we?"

"I'm not sure I'd put it like that—"

"I would. I know that Erik's been waiting a long time to get back at me for the Glencannon thing, and when that bastard Niles Madison gave him a shot, he took it. If I wasn't so ticked off right now, I could almost admire the fact that he's finally about to finesse me. Or so he thinks. The game's not over yet."

Rita was beginning to wish that she'd never heard of Phil Soames; in fact, she wholeheartedly regretted calling him. What can of worms had she inadvertently opened up here? She wanted to tell him that she'd made a mistake and then hang up, but she knew she'd be sorry if she did that. She couldn't let him go without trying to get the whole story out of him.

"And how is he about to do that?" she asked. "Finesse you, I mean."

"How do you think? He went to Chicago to talk to the Sutcliff people, didn't he?"

Rita stiffened. Was that why he'd gone? But Rudy had told her that the client he was meeting was . . . what was the name? She frowned, trying to think. Then she had it. Gelberg. Herbert Gelberg. Mr. Outdoors.

Relieved that Soames was wrong, she said, "No, he went to Chicago to meet with a man named Herbert Gelberg. He's—"

"I know who he is," Soames said. "He and Bob Sutcliff are hand in glove. And they're both cronies . . . beg pardon, I meant, old *fraternity buddies*—" he made the words sound like a curse "—of none other than Niles Madison. Are you getting the picture now, honey?"

Rita was too upset to take umbrage at the condescending term. She tried to say, "But that doesn't mean—"

"Oh, yes, it does. It means that they all went up to that damned lodge of Gelberg's to hammer out some new details about the project. I know how it works. I pulled the same stunt on Erik last year."

Rita's pulse had begun to hammer again. She could hardly get the words out between her stiff lips. "You mean . . . with the Glencannon takeover?"

"Yeah, right," he said. "But that was small potatoes compared to this. I mean, one measly little company—"

She couldn't let that pass. "That takeover destroyed a lot of lives, Mr. Soames. Just because it didn't seem to have any impact on you doesn't mean that other people didn't suffer."

"Oh, but you're wrong—it did have an impact on me. A very favorable one, too, I might add. I doubt Erik ever told you, but I made a lot of money off that deal . . . and he never even saw it coming. It was beautiful, if I do say so myself."

She tensed even more. "Are you telling me that Erik didn't have anything to do with that takeover?"

"Oh, yeah, he had something to do with it. He got in the way, and he got run over. By the time the dust settled and he realized that I'd taken that deal right out from under him—and turned it around to benefit *my* people at Maxwell—it was all over but the funeral."

She was clutching the phone so tightly that her fingers hurt. She switched the receiver to the other hand. Flatly, she said, "I don't believe you."

"Too bad. For once, I'm telling the truth. It's not a usual state of affairs for me, I admit, but hey, a guy can't be truthful all the time or it ruins his reputation, right?"

"From what you've said tonight, I'm sure you don't have to worry about your reputation."

He laughed nastily. "You're probably right. But that's the way it goes in business. One minute you're up, the next you're in the Dumpster."

She was so upset, unnerved and angry that she had to say, "Where you are right now?"

"Yeah, but I won't be there for long," he retorted. "I'm not going to take this lying down—and you can tell Erik that for me. In fact, when you see him, warn him for me that from now on, he'd better be looking over his shoulder every minute. I'm going to be breathing down his neck, and when I get my chance to take him, it won't be pretty."

"I'm not going to tell him that! In fact—"

"Tell him this, then. He can try to put together all the financing he wants, he can pull all the funds away from his existing clients, he can fly off to Chicago to try and make arrangements behind my back, but it's *not* going to work. If he doesn't lay off, he'll regret it. Like he did before. You got that?"

"I've got it," she said. "But here's what I have to say."

"I'm listening."

"If you want any messages delivered to Erik, deliver them yourself."

She hung up before he could reply. But her hands were shaking, and she had to clasp them tightly together. What an awful man! she thought. She had disliked even his voice. But as she stood there, trying to control her trembling, she knew that he'd been telling the truth about the Glencannon takeover—and the Sutcliff project, whatever that was.

He can try to put together all the financing he wants, he can pull all the funds away from his existing clients... but it's not going to work.

She heard Soames's voice in her mind again and thought about what he'd said. Erik could take financing away from his existing clients. Was that what he had done to Grace? But if he had, why? And even more to the point, *how* could he do it? Grace had signed contracts; she and Erik had a deal.

Did that really matter? She'd never forgotten what Erik had told her so callously last year when she'd asked him to explain what had happened. He'd said, "It's just business, Rita. The way things are done. No harm, no foul. Feelings don't enter into it. Why, did you think they did?"

Yes, she'd thought feelings entered into it. But he'd been so cold. He'd actually believed that they could just go on, as though he hadn't completely destroyed everything she'd ever felt for him.

Was that how it was supposed to go this time?

The doorbell sounded suddenly, and she jumped and whirled in that direction. Who could that be? She wasn't expecting company. She wasn't in the mood to see or talk to anyone.

The noise came again before she could move. It was so insistent that she found herself moving toward the door before she could stop herself. She needed some way to vent all this tension, so she reached for the handle and jerked it open, intending to tell whoever was out there to go away.

"Hi," Erik said. "I've been trying to call you all the way from the airport, but your phone's been busy, so I thought I'd just stop by and—" He stopped. "Is something wrong?"

"Yes, something's wrong!" she said shrilly. "Everything is wrong! Who did you go to see in Chicago?"

He looked at her in surprise. "Didn't I tell you? No, I guess I forgot. I went to see one of my clients, a man named Herbert Gelberg."

Her voice shook when she spoke, despite her efforts to control it. "So you said. Who else was there?"

He looked even more astonished. "Why?"

"Because I want to know, that's why!"

He was still standing on the threshold. Since her voice was rising, he said, "Can I come in?"

She tried to calm down. They wouldn't settle anything if she kept yelling at him. "Maybe you'd better," she managed to say between gritted teeth. "We seem to have a few things to discuss."

She didn't wait for him, but whipped around and went into the living room. She stood there, arms folded across her chest, while he shut the door and followed.

"Rita," he said, "what's all this about?"

"You don't know?"

He had the gall to look completely bewildered. "All I know is that when I left, everything was fine. Now I'm back, and you're mad as hell. What happened in the meantime?"

"Well, for one thing, the financing for the store has disappeared."

"What? That's impossible."

"That's what we thought, too. But I went to the bank, and they confirmed the fact that there's no money in the account."

"They made a mistake."

"None that we could find. And believe me, we tried. Do you want to tell me what's going on? Not even Rudy seems to know."

"I don't know, either. But don't worry about it. I'm sure we can—"

"You might as well know, while I was waiting for the bank to figure out what was wrong, I made a few calls."

"And?" He still didn't get it. "Who did you call?"

"Santa Claus and Mickey Mouse, who do you think?" she exclaimed, infuriated by his lackadaisical attitude. "I called your investors, of course. And don't ask me how I got their names. I have my ways."

He stiffened. "I wish you'd asked me first."

"I would have, if you'd been in communication with the rest of the world! As it was, I had to make do on my own!"

"So what did you ask them?"

"I asked them what happened to the damned money, that's what!"

"You had no—" He caught himself in time. Visibly trying to control himself, he said slowly, "All right, you called them. What did they say?"

"Oh, they were very loyal to you, Erik. Either that or you had already worked out your story with them. All they'd say was, 'Ask Erik.' So that's what I'm doing. What happened to that money?"

He was beginning to sound irritated. But whether that was because he genuinely didn't understand what had happened, or because he was irked that she'd gone over his head, she couldn't tell. She didn't care. She was going to get to the bottom of this if they had to stand here all night.

There was an edge to his voice as he said, "I told you, I don't know. There's obviously been a mistake, but just as obviously, I can't do anything about it tonight. I promise I'll talk to the bank the first thing in the morning. Now, was there anything else?"

How could he be so complacent? "You can't talk to the bank tomorrow," she reminded him. "It's Saturday."

"That's not a problem. My people are available at all hours."

"Oh, is that right? Could it be because they might want to discuss the Sutcliff project?"

He went still. "What do you know about that?"

"Not as much as you're going to tell me."

"There's nothing to tell."

She knew he was lying. It was as though he'd shot a bolt through her heart. *Not again!* she thought despairingly, and thrust the thought away. She had to stay with this; later, she'd wonder if he had betrayed her . . . again. Right now she didn't know what was going on—only that he wasn't telling her the truth.

"Oh, really?" she said. "Then you won't be interested in the fact that I just talked to someone named Phil Soames."

Erik's face changed. If she hadn't been so angry herself, she would have been alarmed by the look that came into his eyes when he heard that name. His voice tight, he said, "And? What did *he* have to say?"

"A number of things. We had an interesting conversation."

"I can imagine." With a jerk, he loosened his tie. "Would you mind if I have a drink?"

"Help yourself," she said, vowing that he wasn't going to distract her. "It's in the bar over there. But while you're at it, you can give me an explanation about all this."

He didn't answer but brushed by her toward the little bar in the corner. Her mouth tight, she waited while he searched for and found a bottle of bourbon. She waited while he poured two fingers of liquor into a glass.

"Well?" she demanded.

He turned toward her. "You can't believe anything Phil Soames says. He's a liar and a cheat, he always has been."

"Funny. He says the same thing about you."

"He'd say anything about me if he thought it would benefit him."

"Fine, *you* tell me the truth, then. Did you go to Chicago to meet a client named Gelberg, or were you really there to talk to the people involved in this other project?"

He didn't look at her. "What difference does it make? Neither of them have anything to do with you."

"But that's where you're wrong, Erik. This has everything to do with me. Because, you see, I had a nice little chat with someone else last night. *Her* name was Pamela Madison."

Erik paled. "For God's sake," he muttered. "What did *she* want?"

"To tell me that you and the Madisons are quite a cozy little group these days. To say that you really went to Chicago at the behest of Niles Madison to make a deal with this Sutcliff fellow. And to mention—"

She'd been about to say something about marrying Caroline, but Erik's face turned red, and he stormed, "She's lying to you, Rita. I can't believe you even listened to such—"

"So, are you going to marry Caroline Madison?"

"What? Where did you hear that?"

"Where do you think? Is it true?"

"No, it's not true. For God's sake, Rita—"

He put the glass down and started toward her, but she flung up a hand. "Stay where you are! Don't you dare touch me!"

He stopped. "This is ridiculous! What can I say—"

"For starters, you can tell me who you met with in Chicago."

"Why is it so important to you?"

"Because it is!"

"All right, since you have to know, I did meet with Bob Sutcliff—"

She drew in a breath. "So, Soames *was* telling the truth!"

"No, he wasn't. And how did he know, anyway?"

"What does that matter? It's not even the point!"

He looked at her a moment before he shook his head angrily. "No, I guess it isn't. That's between Phil and me, anyway."

"Let's get back to the subject here. Remember it? You were going to explain why you were at some lodge outside Chicago having a nice little chat with someone named Bob Sutcliff when you were supposed to be here, taking care of Grace's problem with the bank!"

"I didn't know she was having a problem with the bank. But this other thing wasn't my doing, anyway. Herb had invited the guy. I didn't know he was going to be there."

"Oh, how convenient," she said scathingly. "And all you talked about was the weather, right?"

"No, as a matter of fact, we talked about the hotel project."

"And?"

He was angry himself now. "Look, I'm tired of this inquisition. If you don't believe me, there's not much I can do."

"Oh, yes, there is," she flung at him. "You can tell me the truth!"

"I did tell you the truth. Now, leave it alone!"

This was what he had done to her last time. When she had desperately needed him to talk to her, when she had wanted him to be honest with her, he had shut her down. Well, it wasn't going to happen again, she thought. She wouldn't let it.

"I can't leave it alone," she said. "I need to know. Phil said—"

"I don't care what Phil said!" he shouted. "I told you, the man's a liar!"

"And so are you!" she cried. "Phil Soames told me tonight that he was responsible for the Glencannon takeover, not you!"

If she'd dropped a bomb at his feet, she couldn't have generated a more explosive reaction. Before her horrified eyes, Erik seemed to swell with rage. He'd reached for his drink again, intending to toss the whole thing back, but when she mentioned Glencannon, he smashed the glass down so hard on the counter that it shattered, and bourbon and glass flew everywhere.

"I told you," he said, spacing every word with a harsh breath, "that Glencannon is in the past."

Despite what had just happened, she had to say, "For you, maybe. But not for me."

"Why can't you let it go?"

"Because I think it's happening again, only this time it's not Glencannon, it's Sutcliff. You pushed me away before, Erik, but you're not going to do it again. Tell me what really happened. I want to know *now!*"

"And I don't want to talk about that anymore. It's a dead issue. And if you can't let it go, well, then . . ."

"It's not a dead issue with me, Erik. Last year when it happened, you betrayed me—"

He looked at her with angry incredulity. "I didn't *betray* you! For God's sake, Rita, grow up. I told you then, and I'm telling you now, it was just business!"

"Business! You used me!"

He laughed scornfully. "You've been watching too many movies."

She was losing control; she could feel it. She'd had such good intentions; instead of blowing up and making wild accusations, she had promised herself that this time she would listen to what he had to say. They'd talk about what had happened; he would explain his side of it. She would hear him out, they'd make up, and they would go on. What a dreamer she'd been!

Her voice shaking, she said, "Don't you dare deny it. It might have been business to you, but all the time I thought we had something going, you were just using me to get inside information!"

"And just what 'information' do you think you could have told me that would possibly have made a difference?" he asked derisively. He shook his head, infuriating her all the more. "You always did have an inflated opinion of yourself, Rita, but this is too much, even for you. *Inside information.* That's rich!"

She wanted to smack him, to shake him, to scream at him that he was tearing them apart by his stand. But she could only gaze at him, too infuriated to speak. How *dare* he patronize her! Who did he think he was?

She finally managed to force some words out over the lump of fury in her throat. "Let me get this straight," she said. "What you're trying to tell me is that everyone is a liar but you. You want me to believe that *you* were the one responsible for what happened to Mr. Glencannon and all the rest of us who worked at the store. Is that it?"

"That's it," he said. "You wanted the truth? Well, here it is. Phil was in over his head back then. He is now. But he couldn't admit it then, and he can't today."

She looked at him, and suddenly her anger dissolved and was replaced by a sad resignation. She'd wanted a sign; well, here it was. What more did she need to prove that this relationship was all wrong for her, for him, for them both? She should have followed her instincts when they met again, but no, she'd had to give it one nore try.

"I see," she said dully.

"What does that mean?"

"It means that this scene has made it painfully clear that I don't know you as well as I thought. In fact, I believe that I don't know you at all, and never did."

"Look," he said. "It happened. But I can't change it now. Why can't we just put it behind us and go on?"

She couldn't answer for a few seconds. Finally, she was able to say, "The fact that you can ask me that is exactly the reason why it's over between us, Erik. As they say, you just . . . don't . . . get it."

"Rita, please listen—"

But Rita was through listening; she was finished begging for explanations. She walked by him and opened the front door. "I think you should leave now," she said.

He didn't move for a moment. Then, a muscle working in his jaw, he nodded curtly and left. She didn't watch him go down the walk; she didn't listen for the sound of his car driving away. As she shut the door on him, she closed her burning eyes. He was out of her life again, but this time it was for good. She felt so awful that she couldn't even cry.

CHAPTER FIFTEEN

"ARE YOU OUT OF YOUR MIND?" a disbelieving Rudy demanded of Erik on Monday morning. "Why didn't you tell Rita the truth? How could you let her think—"

"I don't know, I don't know, I don't *know!*" Erik muttered, his head in his hands. "I've told you that a dozen times now, so just leave it, will you? I've got a headache the size of Manhattan, and I don't need any lectures from you!"

"No, I won't leave it," Rudy said. "For God's sake, Erik, think about what you're doing here. Think about what you're throwing away!"

Erik had a glass of bicarbonate fizzing on the desk in front of him. Hoping it would do the trick, he grimaced and emptied the glass. The effervescence rose in his stomach, making him feel—if possible—even worse. He glared at Rudy. "I never should have told you that Rita and I quarreled last night. I should have known you'd go on and on about it."

"You're damned right I'll go on about it! Of all the fool things to do—or rather, *not* to do! You should have told her the truth about Glencannon's, Erik. You owed her that."

"I couldn't tell her! Did you really expect me to admit that I was too stupid to figure out what Phil was doing? I have a reputation to consider."

Rudy looked at him incredulously. "You're worried about your reputation when you're about to lose the only woman you've ever really loved?"

"Stop being so damned melodramatic."

"All right," Rudy said, "let's get back to the main problem here. It seems to be your monumental pride. Do you think what happened between you and Phil was a secret? You know how gossip spreads in this business. It was all over town before the ink dried on the deal he made with Jason Maxwell."

Erik had always known that, but he'd refused to face up to it. It had been bad enough to think that a select few had known how he'd been duped; to accept that the entire financial community had been aware of it was a bitter pill to swallow.

More bitter than losing Rita because he couldn't admit he'd made a mistake?

Abruptly, he swiveled the chair around to face the window. "I don't want to talk about it anymore," he muttered. "It's too late now."

"No, it's not," Rudy insisted. "I always knew you were a stubborn so-and-so, Erik. But until now, I never thought you were a fool."

Erik jerked the chair around again. Rudy was standing right beside him. "Either sit down or leave," he said angrily. "You're making me dizzy hovering over me like that. And what do you mean you never thought I was a fool? I certainly proved it last year."

"Anybody could have been caught in that trap. Phil undercut you, Erik, that's all there was to it. He played fast and loose and dirty, to boot. So your pride was hurt, so what? Since you were playing by the rules at the time, you didn't have a chance."

"I should have seen it coming."

"Maybe so, maybe not. But you've let it eat away at you all these months. You're still doing it, but the point is, now you're taking it out on Rita again."

"No, the *point* is that someone offered me the chance to get the better of Phil—"

"Yes, let's talk about that," Rudy interrupted. "You still haven't told me the details of your little meeting with Bob Sutcliff. I thought it was Herb Gelberg who had some kind of emergency."

Erik grimaced. "It seems that the emergency was due to the fact that Bob Sutcliff was flying in to Gelberg's lodge at the behest of none other than Niles Madison."

Rudy sat down abruptly. "I didn't know those three even knew each other."

"Funny thing about that. It seems that they're old fraternity brothers from way back."

"So Sutcliff offered you the project instead of Phil, is that it?"

"That's it."

"What did you tell him?"

"I said I'd have to think about it."

"*Think* about it?" Rudy repeated. He almost levitated out of the chair. "What is there to think about? You know that deal has big strings attached to it. You told me before that Niles Madison has arranged things—or tried to—so that if you get Sutcliff, Caroline gets you. Is that what you really want?"

Erik was losing his temper again, too. "What was I supposed to say, Rudy? When a man like Bob Sutcliff offers you a piece of the action, you can't just say no! Can you imagine the repercussions from that?"

"Don't get cute with me, Erik. That's not why you put him off and you know it. You were trying to figure out how you could get Phil and save your own hide at the same time." Rudy looked at him contemptuously. "Well, you know what? The way you've been acting, I'm surprised there's even a question in your mind. So go ahead—sink to Phil's level and to hell with everything else. It's what you've been wanting to do ever since the damned thing happened last year, so do it!"

"And why not?" Erik demanded. "I've had to do a lot of damage control after Phil practically destroyed my reputation. I've been waiting to get back at him—"

"No," Rudy interrupted, "you've been obsessing on it." He made a disgusted sound. "Don't you think it's time to put it behind you? Don't you think it's time to grow up?"

Erik shot to his feet. Leaning both hands on the desk, he stared down at his partner. "You'd better watch yourself, Rudy," he said.

Rudy wasn't impressed; they'd known each other for too long. "No, you're the one who'd better watch it. Because if you don't, you're going to lose Rita—again. And I don't think you really want to do that."

"You don't know what I want!"

"Neither, it seems, do you."

"I think you'd better get out of my office, Rudy."

Thoroughly repulsed, Rudy stood. "I think you're right. You're obviously not going to listen to reason, so do what you have to do. But don't include me in it. I don't want to be involved in a devil's bargain where you get the prize only if you marry a woman you're not in love with."

His face turning crimson, Erik shouted, "Get out!"

Rudy went.

Breathing hard, Erik threw himself down in his chair again. He was so furious that he wanted to sweep everything off the desk into the trash. He clenched his hands instead.

Rudy was right, he thought. He should have told Rita the truth. Why hadn't he? Because when the time came, he couldn't get the words out. How could he admit that Phil had finessed him on the Glencannon deal? How could he say that Phil had snatched it right out from under him because he was so busy acting the big shot that he didn't even see it coming?

He winced. That sounded bad enough. The fact that he hadn't been able to do anything about it even after he'd found out made it even worse. Rita blamed him for all those people losing their jobs, and even though he hadn't been directly responsible, she was right. If he'd acted sooner, he might have been able to salvage the situation—or at least made it less painful.

But of course, if he'd done his job right in the first place, the hostile takeover would never have happened.

He put his head in his hands again. Now what?

Despite all his other problems, Grace's situation came to mind, and he lifted his head. *His* life was a mess, but at least he could straighten out her problem. Reaching for the phone, he began to make the first of several calls. Within an hour, he had traced the difficulty with the bank to—surprise—Niles Madison. A final call to the bank's chief officer resolved the problem with Grace's account, and after he was assured that the financing was in place again, he sat back a moment. Then he picked up the phone again. His face grim, he dialed the offices of Morton, Madison and Shade.

When a pleasant-voiced secretary answered, he identified himself and asked for Niles.

"One moment, please, Mr. Mulholland."

Niles came on the line two seconds later. "So, Erik," Caroline's father said expansively, "how was your trip to Chicago?"

"Interesting," Erik replied.

Niles chuckled. "I thought it might be. Did you like my little surprise?"

"If you mean, did I enjoy meeting Bob Sutcliff, yes, I did. If you mean, did I accept his—I'm sorry, I should correct that. I mean, *your*—offer to become involved in the hotel project, that's a little more difficult to answer."

"I don't see why," Niles said. "I talked to Bob this morning, and he was very much impressed with you. He'd like you on board, Erik." A pause. "And you know, so would I."

Erik took a deep breath. One section of his mind shouted, *What are you doing?* while another quietly murmured approval. He knew what he was doing was right; the pitiful part was that it had taken him so long to recognize it.

"I'm grateful, Niles," he said. He could just imagine the other man swelling with anticipation at the other end of the line. It was going to be a real pleasure to prick that bubble. "But I have to decline," he added.

There was an ominous silence. Then Niles said, "I'm not sure I heard you right, Erik."

"Shall I repeat myself, then?"

"It's not necessary. But I suggest you should reevaluate your decision. You're walking a dangerous line here, opposing me. Bob and I offered you a great opportunity. If you refuse it, there's a definite likelihood that you won't find much work of any substance from here on after."

"Yes, so you've intimated before, Niles. And if that's your pleasure, you're perfectly welcome to do what you have to. But as far as Caroline is concerned—" He paused deliberately. "I have too much respect for her to be intimidated or manipulated into marrying her."

"Why, you—"

Erik didn't give him a chance to finish the epithet. Calmly, he said, "Goodbye, Niles."

"You'll be sorry!"

Thinking that what he really felt was relief, Erik hung up. He sat there for a few minutes, grinning with satisfaction. Then he thought of Rita, and his smile slipped. Now that he'd taken care of the Madisons, what was he going to do about her?

He was still pondering the best approach when Eleanor buzzed through. "Mr. Bob Sutcliff on line one, Erik."

"That was fast," he said to himself. He could imagine an infuriated Niles burning up the phone lines to contact his old frat brother Sutcliff. Wondering what new threats the two had concocted now, he sat forward and picked up the phone.

"Hello, Bob," he said, "what can I do for you?"

As Erik had discovered at Gelberg's lodge, Bob Sutcliff didn't mince words. In his raspy voice, he said, "I just talked to Niles, and I have to say, he was mighty upset."

"I'm sorry to hear that," Erik said neutrally.

"Well, so am I. Niles and I go back a long way, as you know. But I have to tell you, I never did approve of this carrot-and-stick approach of his. I mean, I tried to tell him that you just can't force a man to marry your daughter—not these days, that is. And I ought to know, because I've got four girls myself. So one reason I'm calling is to tell you that I think you made the right decision. In fact, I would have been disappointed if you'd done anything else.''

Wondering where this was going, Erik said, "Thank you."

"And I'd like to talk to you about something else."

Here it comes, Erik thought. "Go ahead."

"I had my eye on you up there in the woods, and I liked what I saw," Sutcliff told him. "In fact, that's really why I went to Gelberg's lodge. I know Phil Soames is eager to be involved with my project, but I also know I'd have to watch him every minute because he's an unprincipled sort. Now that you and I have had a chance to talk and get to know each other a little, I'd rather have you on board. I'm a great one on character, and after what you've done, I know you've got what it takes. With you, I can do what I need to do and let you get on with your job. So, what do you say? Are you in? No strings attached."

Erik was so stunned he didn't know what to say. "That's quite an offer, Bob," he managed to say. "But I... er... I have some prior commitments to take care of—"

"Well, naturally. I wouldn't expect anything else."

"And of course, I'll have to talk to my partner—"

"Go ahead," Sutcliff said with a laugh. "I'll wait."

Erik laughed, too. In fact, he felt positively giddy. "How about if I call you back at the end of business today?"

"That'll do," Sutcliff said. "I'll be talking to you."

You will indeed, Erik thought. After saying goodbye, he dropped the phone in the cradle and ran down to Rudy's office. Sticking his head in the doorway, he quickly told his partner about Sutcliff's call. He was about to rush off again when Rudy stopped him.

"Wait!" Rudy exclaimed. "Don't you want to talk about this?"

"Later," Erik said, grinning at the thought that they were going to make one of the biggest, most lucrative deals in their career. Rudy stared at him, nonplussed, but he couldn't take more time to explain. He'd pulled off a great coup, but right now he didn't care what Phil Soames was going to think or how he might react, because he had something much more important to take care of.

"But—" Rudy said.

Erik's grin widened as he headed back down the hall. "Later," he said again. "Right now, I've got a call to make."

RITA WAS HAVING A BAD DAY. She had vowed not to involve Grace, but the moment she arrived at work, she tearfully spilled out the story about what had happened between her and Erik.

"I don't know what to do," she finally said, wadding up the handkerchief Grace had given her. "I just don't see a future for our relationship if Erik won't confide in me. But even when I asked him directly if he was responsible for that business with Mr. Glencannon, he denied it."

Tears welled up again as she looked at her sympathetic employer. "If he'd rather I thought him a liar and cheat than someone who just got bested in a business deal, there's no hope for us."

Grace wasn't happy with Erik's behavior, either. But she was older and wiser, and she said, "He's a proud man. Maybe, now that he's had time to think about it, you should give him another chance."

But Rita had already thought about it, too—far into the lonely, empty hours of the night. Dull-eyed, she'd even watched the sun come up, but it hadn't been an uplifting experience. All she could think of was how many days in the future she'd have to face without Erik.

"No," she said. "He's had enough chances. It's just not going to work. I knew that the first time around. I should have listened to my instincts when we met again."

They were sitting on the couch in the apartment, and Grace reached for her hand. Quietly, she said, "But you did listen to your instincts, my dear. And until recently, you were so happy. I'd hate to see you throw all that away."

"*I* didn't throw it away, Erik did. All he had to do was tell me the truth, but he couldn't even do that."

"Sometimes the truth isn't all it's cracked up to be," Grace murmured. "I'm beginning to realize that there are times when it's best to hold a few things back."

Rita didn't agree. How could two people develop the love and trust needed to sustain them in times of trouble if they weren't completely honest with each other?

"I know you mean well—" she started to say.

Grace gave her fingers a squeeze. "I think you need some time to mull things over. Take a week off. Go to the beach, read...do whatever you like. Just getting away will do wonders for your state of mind, I promise."

Rita wasn't sure of that. And she didn't want time off. On the contrary, with her emotions tearing her apart, she needed to dive into as much work as she could find. Anything, she thought mournfully, to keep her mind off Erik.

"I don't want to leave you with all this," she said.

"Nonsense. I'll be perfectly fine on my own. In fact, now that I'm thinking about it, I might even take a day or so away myself. Ever since I came back to San Francisco, I haven't spent as much time with Mallory or my brother as I'd wanted, so this will be a good opportunity. Then, when Erik straightens out this financial mess—"

"*If* he does."

"He will," Grace said confidently. "And in the meanwhile, we'll each have a little holiday. When we get back, I'm sure things will look much brighter."

Since she wasn't sure how they could look much worse, Rita couldn't argue with that. But she was still reluctant to go. "I don't know—"

"I do." Grace stood up, pulling Rita with her. "Now, run along. I'll call you in a few days and tell you where we stand. But remember," she added sternly, "whatever you do, I don't want you to spare a thought about work. It will all be here when we get back."

At that moment, Rita wasn't sure she was going to come back—not if it meant continuing to work with Erik on a regular basis. She knew that after what had happened, she wouldn't be able to see or talk to him, even on a business level. No matter how proud she was of her professionalism, that was too much to expect.

But she hadn't made the actual decision to quit yet, so she said nothing to Grace. Trying not to break into useless tears again at the way things had turned out, she thanked her friend and employer and drove slowly home to her empty house.

BACK AT THE APARTMENT, which was still serving as her office, Grace was trying to decide what to do first when the phone rang. Preoccupied with her address book, she answered and immediately recognized Erik's voice.

"Hello, Grace," Erik said. "I'm calling to tell you that I've handled the problem with the bank. The money is back in your account whenever you want it."

"I knew you'd do it," Grace said. "Did you find out what happened?"

"It was a . . . clerical error."

Erik had been careful, but Grace heard just the tiniest hesitation before he answered, and decided not to pursue it. She suspected that the error had been a little more difficult to straighten out than he'd let on, but it was his job, and she was glad to let him do it. "Now I can call the contractor and tell him to proceed, full steam ahead."

"That you can."

"Was there something else?" she asked.

"Well . . . I was wondering if I could talk to Rita."

"Oh, dear. Rita isn't here. I gave her some time off."

He hesitated. "I hate to involve you, Grace, but . . . was she upset?"

Grace couldn't pretend that she hadn't noticed anything amiss. But she respected Rita's privacy, so she said carefully, "She wasn't her usual self."

"That was my fault. I . . . may I confide in you, Grace?"

"But of course," Grace said, pleased. Over the summer, she realized that she had come to regard Erik as a second son. She didn't know if that was because of her continued estrangement with Gabriel, but perhaps it didn't matter. She felt the same way about Rita, and until recently, she had been entertained by watching her sharp executive assistant and her sophisticated finance man engage in all those silly and romantic age-old rituals of courtship.

What had been even more amusing, she thought, was that they hadn't realized that's what they were doing. Their struggle not to admit their feelings for each other had been delightful to see; it made her think back to the glory days of her relationship with Jeffrey.

Hastily, she abandoned that line of thought. Her relationship with her husband was another problem. Right now, she wanted to help these two.

Erik seemed to be struggling with what he wanted to say. Trying to help him out, she asked, "Was it something about Rita?"

"Yes, it was," he said glumly. "I don't know how much Rita told you, but we had a terrible fight, and it's all my fault."

"Is that so," she said neutrally.

"Yes, first it was about that . . . mix-up at the bank regarding your account. I told her I'd take care of it, but that wasn't good enough. She seemed to think that I'd planned it."

"But you said it was a mistake."

"Yes, it was. *My* mistake. To make a long story short, I recently stepped on some important toes, and this was the man's way of demonstrating his displeasure. It was also a warning of things to come unless I saw the light."

"I'm not sure I like the sound of this."

"I handled it this morning. But Rita is a different story, and I . . . I'm not sure what to do."

"I think the first thing is to decide how you feel about her, Erik."

"I don't have to decide that. I already know. I love her. I want her to be my wife."

Grace felt a silly thrill at the words. Love was so exciting, she thought, even when men persisted in making things as difficult as possible for themselves.

"That's easy enough," she said. "All you have to do is tell her."

"No, that won't be good enough. I know Rita. She would never accept a simple apology."

"I think you underestimate her."

"That would be true if we'd just had a simple little fight or a misunderstanding. But this goes back a long way—to last year, in fact, when Glencannon's was taken over by Maxwell and Company."

"So, what are you going to do about it?"

"I have to tell her the real story."

He knew what he had to do, but his reluctance was obvious. Grace didn't know why, but she suddenly thought of Jeffrey. Smiling sadly, she said, "I think that's a good idea, Erik."

"Will you help me?"

"You know I'll do anything I can."

Typical Erik, she thought fondly, he'd already thought out a plan. "Thank you," he said. "Now, here's what I want you to do. . . ."

CHAPTER SIXTEEN

RITA WAS HOME when Grace called. She'd been so miserable that she hadn't even talked to anyone in her family, especially Marie. She knew her sister would immediately sense that something was wrong, and she couldn't bring herself to discuss what had happened with Erik. She couldn't remember ever being so unhappy, not even the first time they'd split up. All the joy seemed to have gone out of her life; she couldn't even contemplate going back to work.

She knew she couldn't just sit at home, feeling miserable. She had to pull herself together and decide what she was going to do. The problem was, she couldn't think straight. Every time she remembered what she and Erik had said to each other, she wanted to cry. She'd tried so hard to get through to him, but he wouldn't let her in. She loved him deeply, but if he didn't trust her enough to confide in her, it was obvious to her that their relationship had no future.

So the ball was in his court, she thought mournfully, where it seemed about to stay. They'd quarreled on Friday night; it was now Tuesday morning, and the phone hadn't rung once. With every hour that dragged by and she didn't hear from him, her hope that they would work this out became fainter and fainter, until it faded completely.

He's not going to call, she told herself. She had to accept that and get on with her life. She had other things to occupy her: friends, a great job....

Even the thought exhausted her, and she couldn't understand why. Working for Grace was business; being involved with Erik was personal. The two were different things. Just because she and Erik had had a falling out didn't mean she had to give up a dream career with Grace DeWilde. She'd been working toward the position she was in now for years; things were moving along with the store, and even greater opportunities awaited her there. She'd be a fool to allow her feelings to interfere with her career.

And yet...

She'd been so sure that she could handle this. She'd told herself from the beginning that all would be well as long as Erik did his job while she did hers. Well, Erik had done *his* job, she thought. She was the one who had gone wrong. It was up to her to get back on track.

Depressed beyond tears, she was sitting out on the deck, holding a cold cup of coffee in both hands, when the phone rang. Her nerves were so on edge that she almost dropped the cup. She looked blankly at the phone. Should she answer? But what if it was Erik, finally making the call that she had practically willed him to make since they'd quarreled. What was she going to say? How should she act? And why hadn't she thought about her response before now?

She picked up the phone and said hello.

"Good morning," Grace said. "I hoped you'd be home."

"Oh, I'm here, all right." She was in such a blue funk that she wasn't even sure if she was disappointed or not that it was Grace who was calling and not Erik. She sat up. "But I'm surprised that you're calling. I thought you were going to spend some time with your brother and niece."

"Oh, I will. But I'm putting it off for a while because I just had the most wonderful idea."

"Oh?" Rita could tell by Grace's tone that she had thought of something to cheer her up. She knew Grace was concerned about her, and she was grateful, but she didn't want to be inspired. Like a wounded cat, she intended to stay right where she was, feeling sorry for herself and licking her wounds.

"Yes," Grace went on blithely. "It's been a long time since I've visited Lake Tahoe, so I thought I'd take a few days and go up there. I was wondering if you'd like to come with me."

She didn't want to go anywhere, even with Grace. "Oh, Grace, I don't think—"

"Please, Rita. It would be good for you, and it would make me so happy. We could go up for a couple of days, see a show or two, maybe do a little gambling, eat until we're stuffed, and then come home again, ready to start work. What do you think? Doesn't it sound wonderful?"

Rita couldn't imagine anything she'd like to do less— except maybe clean the underside of her car with a toothbrush. Besides, she was suspicious of Grace's lively tone; it wasn't like her to be so...jovial.

"It sounds like a great idea," she said carefully, "but I don't think I'd be good company. I'm not in the best of moods right now."

"But that's just the point," Grace persisted. "We have to get you out of these doldrums, and what better way than doing something spontaneous and totally out of the ordinary? It will be fun."

With Grace being so uncharacteristically insistent, Rita didn't see how she could refuse. Hoping she didn't sound as reluctant as she felt, she said, "Well . . . I suppose a few days wouldn't hurt."

"That's the spirit! Now, you don't have to worry about a thing, because I'm going to take care of all the details. When can you be ready?"

Just the thought of packing made her feel infinitely weary. "I guess I could go tomorrow or the next day."

"What's wrong with today? I don't want to give you time to think of an excuse, so I'll pick you up about noon. Is that too soon?"

"Too soon?" She glanced at the kitchen clock. "That's only two hours away!"

"I know," Grace said with a laugh. "But remember, we're going to be spontaneous. I'll see you soon!"

As soon as she heard the dial tone in her ear, Rita wanted to call Grace back. This was ridiculous, she thought. She didn't want to go to Lake Tahoe. She didn't want to go around the block. Then she reconsidered. Grace was right: she couldn't stay here and vegetate. And Grace was her employer. Spending time together outside of work might prove to be beneficial for both of them.

Two hours didn't give her much time, but as Rita trudged around her bedroom, tossing things into a small suitcase, she decided that she didn't need a whole lot of time, anyway. She wasn't going to be seeing anyone she knew except Grace at Lake Tahoe; for all anyone cared, she could go around in torn jeans and an old T-shirt. But then she remembered that Grace had mentioned something about going out to dinner and to a show, so she sighed and packed two good dresses. She didn't feel like partying, but she couldn't go to a nightclub act as if she'd just gotten off the bus.

Grace arrived in a pearl gray stretch limousine exactly at twelve. Wearing a dark suit, white shirt and conservative tie, the chauffeur jumped out, took Rita's bag and smartly opened the door for her. She'd barely climbed inside and settled herself before they were off, pulling smoothly away from the curb and heading toward 101 North.

The limo had been stocked with every goody imaginable, including champagne on ice. "I know it's early in the day, but I thought we'd celebrate," Grace said as she poured two flutes. She held out one for Rita.

Rita took the glass. "What are we celebrating?"

"Oh, I don't know," Grace said gaily. "How about the fact that it's a beautiful day, and we're on our way for a few days of vacation?"

Grace looked so happy and pleased with herself that Rita didn't want to disappoint her. With a weak smile, she clinked her glass with Grace's and took a sip of the excellent bubbly wine. It tickled her nose and throat, and she was just thinking how good it tasted when she remembered a never-opened bottle she'd bought for a liaison with Erik. She put the glass aside.

Once they were out of the city and heading toward Sacramento, the drive to South Shore, Lake Tahoe, took about three hours, with time added for a lunch stop along the way. It was four o'clock when they came around a mountain curve on Highway 50 and saw the deep sapphire waters of the famous lake far below them. It was such a beautiful, peaceful sight that Rita began to relax despite herself. She was just thinking that this might not have been such a bad idea when Grace found the videotape.

"What's this?" Grace murmured, turning it over. She looked up in surprise. "Look at this. It says, 'Play Me.'"

"Cute," Rita said. "Just like *Alice in Wonderland.*"

"Maybe we should play it."

"Go ahead, if you want to," Rita said indifferently. "But it's probably just a promotional tape for the limousine company. After all—" she gestured toward the small color TV mounted over the little bar "—we're a captive audience, aren't we?"

"Captive or not, we still have a while before we arrive. I'm going to put it in the machine."

Grace took the videotape out of its box and inserted it into the VCR on top of the little TV. Two seconds later, when a familiar countenance filled the screen, Rita realized that it wasn't a promotional tape—not for the limousine company, anyway.

"What in the world—" she exclaimed when she saw Erik's face. She looked accusingly at Grace. "Did you know about this?"

Grace returned her look serenely. "Why don't we just listen to what he has to say?"

Erik, it seemed, had plenty to say. Wearing a navy blue suit and tie, he stood before a plain black backdrop and appeared to be staring right into Rita's eyes. As though he knew where Grace was sitting, he glanced to the right and said, "Thanks, Grace. I owe you for this."

Rita turned to her boss again. "You *were* in on it!"

"Just listen," Grace said.

Rita jerked back to face the TV. She didn't know whether to obey Grace's admonition or to switch the VCR off because she'd been tricked. She wanted to do the latter, but she couldn't seem to make her arm reach out. As Grace had said, all she could do was listen.

"I know you're angry, Rita," Erik went on. "And you have good reason to be. That's why I chose this method of trying to explain what happened instead of calling you or trying to see you. I wasn't sure you would listen to me—"

"You're right about that," Rita muttered.

"Shh," Grace said.

Gazing right into the camera, Erik continued. "You wanted to know what happened with Glencannon's, Rita, so here's the story. Phil did engineer that takeover. And he did it without me finding out about it—until it was too late to do anything about it."

"So Soames *was* telling the truth!" Rita exclaimed.

Painfully, Erik went on. "The plain fact is that Phil outsmarted me, Rita. When it counted, he was more clever than I was...and more ruthless. When I found out what he'd done, I tried to stop it. But he'd convinced the board at Maxwell and Company that they'd be better off absorbing Glencannon's than forming a partnership. I argued until I was blue in the face. I proved he was wrong with facts and figures. But they were too dazzled by the profits Phil had convinced them were there for the taking to listen to me. I know they've since discovered their mistake, but only, of course, when it was too late."

Rita sat back. Now she knew why Gerald Hastings had been so hysterical at her idea of the bridal boutique. The store had been steadily losing money; they just didn't have the financial resources for it. It wasn't that it was a bad idea; it was that it was too expensive.

"Oh, Erik," she murmured.

He wasn't finished. "I couldn't tell you this before, Rita, for several reasons. Rudy thinks it's because I've been too proud to admit that I'd been bested—and that's true, as far as it goes. But what even Rudy doesn't know is how hurt I was that Phil could do something like that to me. You see, Phil and I were once best friends...."

He paused, and a brief, regretful smile flitted across his handsome face. "You have to understand how it was, Rita. We were more than best buddies. We got our first haircuts together, we went out on our first date together. We were inseparable—more like brothers than just friends. In fact, when we were ten, we took a blood oath always to be together. We planned on being business partners—"

The smile faded. "But it didn't work out that way. Something happened to Phil when we got out of college. He started to grow further and further away from me, until I didn't seem to know him at all. But even so, I never thought he would do what he did to me over the Glencannon thing. It was like being stabbed in the back by your twin."

He stopped and glanced down, as if he needed to collect himself. At that moment, he looked so unhappy and forlorn that Rita's already-overflowing heart went out to him. It hadn't been so simple after all, she thought, and was ashamed that she hadn't realized it before. She knew how complex Erik was. She should have sensed that his extreme reluctance to talk about the Glencannon takeover went much deeper than an involvement in a business deal.

Erik looked into the camera again. "I know I should have told you this before, Rita. I wish I had. But some things take longer than others to accept, and it wasn't until I realized that I could lose you—again—that I knew I had to try and explain. Please forgive me."

"I do," Rita whispered. "Oh, I do!"

The tape ended, and she sat there for a moment blinking back joyful tears before she turned suddenly to Grace. "I want to go back," she said. "I have to see Erik, right now!"

"But my dear," Grace protested, "we're almost at the South Shore!"

"I don't care. I know I promised to spend a few days up here with you, but surely you can understand how important it is to me to—"

She stopped. She'd been so involved in what Erik had said on the tape that she hadn't noticed Grace's air of excitement until now. During the two months they'd known each other, Grace had been unfailingly calm and controlled; in fact, Rita couldn't remember her employer ever becoming agitated, no matter what had happened.

But she was animated now, laughing aloud. For a moment, Rita thought that it was because she had helped Erik pull this off, but then she realized that Grace was pointing to something outside the car. While Erik's tape had been running, the limousine had purred down the mountain; they had emerged onto the flat and were heading toward the looming casinos at the state line. Billboards lined the road, and Grace cried, "Look at that!"

Rita didn't want to look. She wanted to convince Grace to turn the car around and go back to San Francisco. Or, failing that, to take her to the airport and she'd fly back by herself.

"Grace—"

"Look!"

"I don't—" she started to say. Then she saw what was on the billboard, and her mouth dropped open.

The sign read, There Comes a Time in a Man's Life When He Suddenly Realizes How Much He's Sacrificed to His Work...

"It must be some kind of advertisement for a new show," she said. She had more important things on her mind, and she turned to Grace again, ready to highjack the car if they didn't turn around.

"I don't think it's an advertisement," Grace said. "Or at least, not the kind you mean. Look at that one!"

They were passing another billboard. This one read, When He Realizes that He's Alone and Likely to Stay that Way Unless He Changes a Few Things...

"If it's some kind of PR campaign," Rita said impatiently, "it doesn't seem to be making its point. Grace—"

"I'm not so sure. There's another one!"

"I don't care! Grace, please listen to me—"

"Look!"

It seemed that there was no other way to get Grace's attention, so she turned to look again. They were just going by a third sign, which read, When He Looks in the Mirror and Knows that It's Time to Settle Down...

Rita frowned. "I don't—"

Grace just smiled. She pointed again. "There's another one."

Rita moved to the edge of her seat. They were coming upon another huge billboard. This one read, Because He's Met the Woman of His Dreams—Twice. Once, He Let Her Get Away. If It Happens a Second Time, He's a Bigger Fool than He Already Knew...

Rita blinked. "That sounds like—" She turned to Grace, who was smiling broadly.

"What do you think, my dear? You wanted an explanation and an apology, didn't you?"

"Yes, but . . . but not a public one—"

"No? Well, perhaps you should have told him that before he went to all this trouble."

They were almost at the South Shore now, where one huge casino after another lined the main road. Vast billboards of every kind and description towered over them, but even before a smiling Grace pointed once more, Rita's glance found the one meant for her. It read, I Promise Never to Keep Anything from You Again.

Rita's heart was pounding; the lump in her throat was too big to let her speak. She had never loved Erik more than she did at this moment. This most private of private men had not only bared his soul to her but to the entire world. She knew how much that had cost him.

She had to see him, she thought again. She had to go back. Urgently, she turned to Grace, but before she could say anything, Grace pointed again. Another big sign came into view.

It read, I Love You, Rita Shannon. Will You Be My Wife?

Rita's hand went to her mouth. "He wants me to marry him. . . ."

"And more," Grace said. "Take another look."

There were other words below the proposal. When she was finally able to read them through her tears, she started to laugh. So small she could hardly see it was the vow: I Promise to Do All the Cooking. And I Won't Go Off with the Men at Family Picnics.

The limousine made a turn and pulled into a driveway. Rita was brushing the tears from her cheeks when she felt the car stop. "Not another billboard!"

Grace gestured. "No, this time I think it's the real thing."

Rita whirled around and looked in the direction Grace was pointing. They'd stopped in front of a wedding chapel, and standing outside, looking nervous and worried and ready to jump out of his skin, was the man she loved. Without waiting for the chauffeur to get out and open the door, she wrenched the handle herself.

"Erik!" she cried, flying toward him. "Oh, Erik, I don't know what to say!"

He scooped her up into his arms. Holding her tightly, he gazed down into her face. Trembling in every limb, he said, "Just say yes. That's all I ask."

And Rita, who had always vowed that she would *never* get married, no matter *what,* looked up at him and without hesitation said, "Yes. Oh, yes. Yes, yes, yes!"

Their lips met in a fiery kiss. It was a few moments before they broke apart, and Rita was still gasping when she remembered Grace. Turning to her friend and employer, she accused with a giddy laugh, "You were in on this all along, weren't you."

Grace's cheeks were pink with delight. "Yes, I was," she said, giving them both a hug. "I hope you don't mind, Rita, but I couldn't resist."

"I don't mind at all. I think it's wonderful. I think you're wonderful—both of you!"

She suddenly realized they were standing in front of the wedding chapel. She was so ecstatic that she was almost tempted to go inside, but then she thought of her family, who had to be present for such a momentous occasion as her marriage. She thought of Grace, who had done so much for her, and who had been so disappointed by her son's elopement. She was so deliriously happy herself that she wanted everyone to feel the same way, and suddenly she knew how to bring all that about.

"Erik," she said, "as much as I'd like to go into that chapel right now, I think it would be a shame if we didn't do it up right, don't you?"

Erik looked pleased and a little alarmed at the same time. Pretending to groan, he said, "Don't tell me you want a *big* wedding."

"The biggest," she answered with a grin. "I want dresses and tuxes and special guests. I want flowers and food and champagne and everything there is. And, Grace, if it's not too much to ask, will you help me plan it?"

Grace didn't answer for a moment. She didn't have to; the look on her face said it all. It was the first time— and probably the last, Rita thought—that she would ever see tears in Grace DeWilde's eyes.

"I'd be honored, my dears," Grace said, reaching for both their hands. "Just tell me when."

Rita looked up at Erik with mischief in her dark eyes. "Since men are so good at handling all these little details," she said, "why don't *you* choose the time and the date?"

"I'll show you how simple it is," he said, pulling her close. "I don't care where or when. Just make it *soon*, all right?"

And so, right there in full view of everyone, with passing cars honking like mad, and Grace looking on like a proud mother hen, they sealed the bargain with another passionate kiss.

WEDDINGS BY DeWILDE

continues with

DRESSED TO THRILL

by Kate Hoffmann

Available in June

Here's a preview!

"So, HAVE YOU ADJUSTED to the fact that you're now DeWilde's new merchandising manager?" Sloan DeWilde asked.

"I'm still a bit overwhelmed," Chloe replied, and paused. "Why *did* I get this job?" she asked finally, a hesitant catch in her voice.

He glanced over at her to find her face cast in a luminous light coming from somewhere behind him.

"Because you're the most qualified," he said, his voice nearly dying in his throat. "And I needed someone I could trust."

At first she looked surprised, and then she smiled. "Then it didn't have anything to do with—" she groped for the right word "—us?"

He grinned. "Us? I thought there was no us."

"You know what I mean. This...obsession you have with me and...fine dining. I thought you might have promoted me just so you could..."

"I promoted you because you're the best person for the job. That's it. There's nothing more."

She sighed. "It's just that if you did have ulterior motives, I was prepared to turn the promotion down."

"Oh, believe me, I still have ulterior motives where you're concerned," he teased. "They just don't have anything to do with your promotion."

Sloan took a step toward her, staring down into her eyes. Slowly, he bent and brushed his lips along hers, lingering for a moment before pulling back.

"Please don't," she said breathlessly, avoiding his gaze.

He kissed her again, this time with more conviction. At first she didn't react, but then he felt her soften in his arms and her lips parted slightly. He pressed her gently into his body as his tongue rimmed her mouth, softly probing, tasting, savoring. "Why not?" he asked. "There's nothing standing in our way."

Slipping his hands around her tiny waist, Sloan slowly backed her against a Queen Anne table filled with beaded white pocketbooks. With a sweep of his hand, he cleared a spot, the pocketbooks tumbling to the floor around his feet. Then he gently lifted her up and placed her in front of him. Her short skirt rode high on her thighs and he stepped between her legs, deepening his kiss. His mouth never left hers while his hands fumbled to free her hair.

"We can't deny this any longer, Chloe," he murmured against her lips as hairpins dropped to the floor. "We don't have to. We're two adults. We can handle this."

"I don't know," Chloe said. "Every instinct tells me this is a mistake. We shouldn't do this."

He furrowed his fingers through her hair, working at the hairpins, tugging softly until she was forced to look up at him. "Why? Give me one good reason."

"I—I don't..." She drew a shaky breath.

"You don't have a reason. Chloe, give me a chance. Let me show you that this can work. Forget the damn store. Forget who I am. All we have to worry about is you and me. No one else."

HARLEQUIN®

Don't miss these Harlequin favorites by some of our most distinguished authors!
And now, you can receive a discount by ordering two or more titles!

HT #25663	THE LAWMAN by Vicki Lewis Thompson	$3.25 U.S.☐/$3.75 CAN. ☐
HP #11788	THE SISTER SWAP by Susan Napier	$3.25 U.S.☐/$3.75 CAN. ☐
HR #03293	THE MAN WHO CAME FOR CHRISTMAS by Bethany Campbell	$2.99 U.S.☐/$3.50 CAN. ☐
HS #70667	FATHERS & OTHER STRANGERS by Evelyn Crowe	$3.75 U.S.☐/$4.25 CAN. ☐
HI #22198	MURDER BY THE BOOK by Margaret St. George	$2.89 ☐
HAR #16520	THE ADVENTURESS by M.J. Rodgers	$3.50 U.S.☐/$3.99 CAN. ☐
HH #28885	DESERT ROGUE by Erin Yorke	$4.50 U.S.☐/$4.99 CAN. ☐

(limited quantities available on certain titles)

	AMOUNT	$
DEDUCT:	10% DISCOUNT FOR 2+ BOOKS	$
ADD:	POSTAGE & HANDLING	$
	($1.00 for one book, 50¢ for each additional)	
	APPLICABLE TAXES**	$_____
	TOTAL PAYABLE	$_____
	(check or money order—please do not send cash)	

To order, complete this form and send it, along with a check or money order for the total above, payable to Harlequin Books, to: **In the U.S.:** 3010 Walden Avenue, P.O. Box 9047, Buffalo, NY 14269-9047; **In Canada:** P.O. Box 613, Fort Erie, Ontario, L2A 5X3.

Name:_____

Address: _____ City:_____

State/Prov.:_____ Zip/Postal Code:_____

**New York residents remit applicable sales taxes.
  Canadian residents remit applicable GST and provincial taxes.   HBACK-JS3

Look us up on-line at: http://www.romance.net

FIVE UNIQUE SERIES
FOR EVERY WOMAN YOU ARE...

♥ *Silhouette* ROMANCE™

From classic love stories to romantic comedies to emotional heart tuggers, Silhouette Romance is sometimes sweet, sometimes sassy—and always enjoyable! Romance—the way you always knew it could be.

SILHOUETTE® *Desire*®

Red-hot is what we've got! Sparkling, scintillating, *sensuous* love stories. Once you pick up one you won't be able to put it down...only in Silhouette Desire.

Silhouette SPECIAL EDITION®

Stories of love and life, these powerful novels are tales that you can identify with—romances with "something special" added in! Silhouette Special Edition is entertainment for the heart.

SILHOUETTE·INTIMATE·MOMENTS®

Enter a world where passions run hot and excitement is always high. Dramatic, larger than life and always compelling—Silhouette Intimate Moments provides captivating romance to cherish forever.

♥ SILHOUETTE YOURS TRULY™

A personal ad, a "Dear John" letter, a wedding invitation... Just a few of the ways that written communication unexpectedly leads Miss Unmarried to Mr. "I Do" in Yours Truly novels...in the most fun, fast-paced and flirtatious style!

SILHOUETTE® *Desire*

Do you want…

Dangerously handsome heroes

Evocative, everlasting love stories

Sizzling and tantalizing sensuality

Incredibly sexy miniseries like **MAN OF THE MONTH**

Red-hot romance

Enticing entertainment that can't be beat!

You'll find all of this, and much *more* each and every month in **SILHOUETTE DESIRE.** Don't miss these unforgettable love stories by some of romance's hottest authors. Silhouette Desire—where your fantasies will always come true….

DES-GEN

HARLEQUIN ⬥ PRESENTS®

HARLEQUIN PRESENTS
men you won't be able to resist falling in love with...

HARLEQUIN PRESENTS
women who have feelings just like your own...

HARLEQUIN PRESENTS
powerful passion in exotic international settings...

HARLEQUIN PRESENTS
intense, dramatic stories that will keep you turning
to the very last page...

HARLEQUIN PRESENTS
The world's bestselling romance series!